W

A Hen
in the
Wardrobe

This book is dedicated to Ardjouna Bouchareb,
and to her son – who found a hen in the wardrobe,
left a sheep in our kitchen and helped me find
'the best of all possible worlds'.

JANETTA OTTER-BARRY BOOKS

A Hen in the Wardrobe copyright © Frances Lincoln Limited 2012
Text and illustrations copyright © Wendy Meddour 2012

The right of Wendy Meddour to be identified as the author and illustrator
of this work has been asserted by her in accordance with the Copyright,
Designs and Patents Act, 1988 (United Kingdom).

First published in Great Britain and in the USA in 2012 by
Frances Lincoln Children's Books, 4 Torriano Mews,
Torriano Avenue, London NW5 2RZ
www.franceslincoln.com

A catalogue record for this book is available from the British Library.

ISBN 978-1-84780-225-5

Illustrated with line and wash

Set in Charis SIL

Printed and bound by CPI Group (UK) Ltd, Croydon, CR0 4YY
in December 2011

1 3 5 7 9 8 6 4 2

A Hen
in the
Wardrobe

J
FIC
meddour
2012.

Wendy Meddour

F

FRANCES LINCOLN
CHILDREN'S BOOKS

A Bump in the Night

All was quiet in Cinnamon Grove. The little cluster of grey terraced houses huddled together beneath the moonlight. Birds tucked their heads under their wings, flowers closed their petals and children snuggled into their duvets like caterpillars in cocoons. Only the brook that gurgled along the bottom of the gardens interrupted the sleepy silence. Everything was drifting into the deep hush of night.

Suddenly there was a CRASH at Number Thirty-two! An upstairs light came on, a door swung open and a man in blue-and-white stripy pyjamas hurtled across the landing. He burst into a bedroom at the top of the stairs and opened the doors of a big white wardrobe. Then, with one swift jerk, he stuck his head inside!

"What's up, Dad?" shouted Ramzi, throwing aside his bedcovers.

"*Where's* it gone?" whispered Dad. He twisted his neck first to the left, then to the right.

"Where's *what* gone, Dad?" Ramzi asked nervously.

But Dad stared straight through Ramzi. His eyes were watery and distant, his dark hair ruffled and unkempt. He stroked his beard and thrust his head back inside the wardrobe. Then he started hurling clothes into the air!

"Stop it, Dad!" cried Ramzi. "You're acting really strange." He ducked to avoid a shower of socks.

"I *will* find it!" said Dad.

"Find *what*?" asked Ramzi, clutching his knees tightly to his chest.

"Here, chicky-chick. Come on, my little hen. I *know* you're in there." Suddenly Dad crawled inside the wardrobe and shut the doors. There was a scratching noise. Then everything went quiet.

Ramzi rubbed his eyes and looked around the room. Clothes were scattered everywhere. He waited. Nothing happened. Ramzi tiptoed across the room and gently opened the wardrobe doors. Dad was sitting cross-legged in the corner, blinking like a startled rabbit.

"Dad, what *are* you doing?" asked Ramzi.

"Where am I?" whispered Dad.

"You're in my wardrobe, Dad! In my bedroom!"

"Huh? Is that you, Ramzi? What time is it?
Where's your mother?"

Ramzi looked at the clock. "It's really late, Dad.
Mum will be back next week. But can you get out
of my wardrobe? This is completely, totally weird."

7

Dad staggered to his feet, scratched his head and looked around.

"But... I don't... understand..." he stammered.

"It's all right, Dad. Come on," said Ramzi gently.

Dad slumped against Ramzi's shoulders and they stumbled back across the landing. Then Ramzi tucked Dad into bed, kissed him lightly on the forehead and turned off the light.

Wake Up!

Next morning, the sun flickered in the sky like a big yellow dandelion. The birds had sung their dawn chorus and flown off on the breeze. The milkman had delivered the milk and gone home for a cup of tea. The postman had finished his round and was doing a crossword in his van. But at Number Thirty-two, the day had not begun. Ramzi and his dad were still fast asleep.

"*Dingaling, Dingaling,*" went the doorbell.

Dad jumped out of bed, splashed his face with water, hopped into his trousers and threw a crisp white shirt on his back. Then he flew down the stairs and opened the door.

An immaculate-looking woman wearing bright pink glasses and matching lipstick stood outside.

"Good morning, Miss Blunt. Can I help you?" puffed Dad.

"It's Miss Sharp, actually," snapped the lady. Her voice was thin and wiry. "And I'm afraid this is *not* a social call. Mr Ramadan – do you realise that this is the *third time* Ramzi has been late for school this week? It's really *not* good enough, you know."

Dad frowned. Then he took a deep breath and looked at the sky. "The sun is shining and the birds are singing. Yes – this is the best of all possible worlds," he sighed.

Miss Sharp screwed her lips together. Mr Ramadan had such a *curious* way of talking. She peered round his shoulders and looked inside. Shoes were scattered in the hall and there was *no* sign of Ramzi or Mrs Ramadan!

"If Ramzi is not in school by ten o'clock this morning," she said, wagging her finger, "then I will report you to..."

Suddenly Ramzi appeared in the doorway.

His skin shone in the sunlight as he rubbed his eyes sleepily.

"Morning, Miss," he grinned.

Miss Sharp gasped! Ramzi's usually neat brown curls stuck up in all directions and his school shirt looked like a crumpled sheet.

"R...R...Ramzi!" she stammered. "Wh...wh... where's your mother?"

"Oh, she's not here, Miss. She's gone to learn about buildings and stuff," said Ramzi cheerfully.

Dad puffed out his chest and smiled proudly. "My wife is training to be an architect, Miss Sharp. Currently, she's studying Domes of the East." His hands fluttered in the air as he spoke.

"*I see*," said Miss Sharp slowly. "Well, in that case, Mr Ramadan, can you *please* make sure that Ramzi gets to school *on time*!" She tapped her watch fiercely. Then, turning on her pointy pink heels, she tottered up the path and out of sight.

"What a dreadful woman!" muttered Dad.

"Dad! You *can't* say that!" giggled Ramzi.

Dad smiled and looked down at his son. "Arggghhhhhh!" he yelled, leaping backwards.

Ramzi jumped. "What? What's up now?"

"Your uniform! Your hair! Your... you're such a mess!" cried Dad.

"But it's not my fault, Dad. It was *you* that messed up all my clothes last night."

Dad looked blank.

"You know...when you were looking for that hen."

"A hen? What hen?"

"The hen in my wardrobe."

"Ramzi, you must *always* tell the truth," said Dad, wiggling his finger at the ceiling. "Remember, the Creator sees all!"

"I *know,* Dad. I completely *am* telling the truth! Last night, you *were* looking for a hen in my wardrobe. Remember?"

There was a pause. Dad's butter-beige cheeks turned grey.

"Are you sure?" he asked.

Ramzi nodded.

"A hen, you say?" Dad slumped on to the bottom stair and put his head in his hands. "Ramzi," he began slowly, "is this the *first* time you've noticed

12

me doing... strange things in the night?"

"Ermm. Well, no, errrmm... not really the absolutely first time, Dad."

Dad looked at Ramzi through the splayed fingers of one hand. "I think you'd better tell me everything, son," he whispered.

Ramzi slowly remembered the previous nights. "Well, two nights ago you were chasing frogs in the pantry... And on the night Mum left, I found you in the bath..."

"Stop!" cried Dad.

There was silence. A car passed by the house, its engine rattling like a faulty washing machine. The fridge hummed loudly in the kitchen.

At last Dad spoke. "Come here, little warrior. I must've frightened you." He swept Ramzi into his big arms and squeezed him tight.

"It's OK, Dad! Really, I'm fine," spluttered Ramzi.

Dad ruffled Ramzi's hair and sighed a deep sigh. Then he looked at his watch. "Oh! It's nearly ten o'clock! Quick, we must get you to school."

Minutes later, they were driving along in the car. An espresso cup teetered on the edge of the dashboard and Ramzi was swigging from a carton of milk.

"One thing, Ramzi," said Dad, clunking into fourth gear. "What did I say I was doing in the bath?"

"Ermm, something about 'sailing to the moon,'" answered Ramzi.

"Oh, no," groaned Dad, "I'm afraid it's *all* starting again!"

A Moonlit Meeting

By the time the school bell rang for lunch, Ramzi was tired and fed-up. He slouched over to a tree that grew in a forgotten corner of the playground and slumped down against its bark. Then he closed his eyes. Red and orange shadows danced under his eyelids as the sunlight shone through the leaves.

He was mid-yawn when a tiny little girl came skipping over. It was Shaima Stalk. Ramzi kept his eyes tightly shut and pretended to be asleep.

"Ahem!" coughed Shaima.

Ramzi ignored her.

"AHEM!" she tried again.

Ramzi opened one eye. "What do you want?" he asked. He didn't usually talk to girls.

"Well, I couldn't help but notice that you're *not* playing football."

"So?" grunted Ramzi.

"Well, it's just that you *always* play football."

"Yeh – well, I don't actually want to."

"Exactly!" said Shaima, pushing her spectacles back up her nose. "And that's how I know."

"Know what?" asked Ramzi.

"Know that *something* or *someone* has been waking you up in the night." She looked like a detective on the trail of a new case.

"What else do you know, Smartypants?" asked Ramzi.

Shaima grinned. "I know that Benjamin Butley's got nits... Miss Sharp wears a wig... Headmaster Gripe keeps his teeth in a drawer..."

Ramzi sniggered.

"And Ramzi Ramadan's missing his mum."

"That's completely *not* true!" shouted Ramzi. "I am *not* missing my mum!" His face crinkled into a scowl.

Shaima twisted some daisies around her fingertips and looked the other way. "But I'm right about the other stuff, aren't I?" A perfectly symmetrical cube of daisies dangled from her hand.

"Wow! How did you do that?" exclaimed Ramzi.

"Oh, it's nothing." She tossed it aside. "Look, you don't *have* to tell me if you don't want to. But it's something to do with your dad, isn't it?"

Ramzi's mouth dropped open. "Wow!" he said again. This girl was different. She was *interesting*.

Shaima's eyes twinkled. She loved being right.

"If you tell me what's up, I promise not to tell *anyone*," she whispered.

Ramzi tugged at the grass. "All right then," he said. "But it's totally, dead secret."

Shaima nodded until her plaits shook.

Ramzi took a deep breath and began. "Since Mum's been away, my dad's been acting really weird..." He scanned the playground to check no one was listening. "The first time it happened, he was chasing frogs in the pantry. Then he tried to sail to the moon in the bath. And last night…"

Shaima leant closer to listen.

"Last night," whispered Ramzi, "he was looking for *a hen in my wardrobe*!"

Shaima's eyes sparkled. "I've read all about this!" she cried. "It must be a case of somnambulism."

Ramzi stared at her blankly.

"What I mean is," Shaima whispered, "your dad's a *somnambulist*."

"No, he's not, actually," said Ramzi. "He's a web designer. I thought you said you were *always* right?"

Shaima sighed. It wasn't easy being a child genius! "No, silly, you don't understand. A somnambulist is a sleepwalker. Your dad's a sleepwalker. He walks in his sleep!"

"No, he doesn't," said Ramzi. "He *runs* and *talks* and *throws* things about."

"Yeah – sleepwalkers do that too. But I've never seen one in action. It must be thrilling!"

"You wouldn't say that if it was *your* dad," snapped Ramzi.

Shaima blushed. She knew Ramzi was right. Her dad got the giggles whenever he ate chocolate and it was *so* embarrassing. They sat in silence and watched the other children race across the playground.

"I know," said Shaima at last. "Let's watch your dad tonight and check he really *is* sleepwalking. Then, when we're sure, we'll find him a special doctor."

"What? A *sleepwalking* doctor?" Ramzi raised an eyebrow.

"Why not?" said Shaima. "You get doctors for everything. My Nanna's got one who just looks at her feet."

"Yuck!" laughed Ramzi, making a face. "OK then. Meet me in my back garden at 11 o'clock tonight."

"Awesome," said Shaima. She picked up her skipping rope and hop-scotched at high speed across the playground.

"But I haven't even told you where I live yet," yelled Ramzi.

"It's OK," called Shaima, "I already know!"

Ramzi lent back against the bark, closed his eyes and smiled. Perhaps tomorrow he would get a good night's sleep?

Looking for Bugs

The moon hung over Cinnamon Grove – a twinkling lantern in the night. Underneath its glow, something scurried across the road and disappeared into the shadows. An owl flung its heavy wings across the sky, spindly-legged spiders wove their silver traps and Shaima waited in the darkness.

It had been easy to sneak out of the house. Shaima's dad was working late at *The Spice Pot*. Her big brother was boarding at *Greystone's Academy for the Bright and Gifted*. Her little brother was fast asleep upstairs and Nanna Stalk and Mrs Stalk were watching the news. The drone of the television echoed through the walls, so no one heard when Shaima tiptoed out of the front door.

She was wearing a dark-green hooded anorak and a pair of black school pumps. The anorak was far too long and hung round her ankles like a tent.

Feeling her way in the darkness, she skulked along the pavement in the shadows.

There were still no lights on at Number Thirty-two. So Shaima opened the gate, crept into the back garden and hid amongst the trailing wisteria. Then she took a torch out of her pocket and waited.

Dddrrrrring! The alarm clock rattled under the pillow. Ramzi's arm shot out from the covers and switched on the globe nightlight. Blue and green patterns danced across the map-covered wall. Ramzi jumped out of bed, threw on a sweater, grabbed a torch and padded across the landing. Dad's bedroom door was ajar. Ramzi peered in.

Chooaah...ssshhh...chooaah...ssshhh! Dad was snoring softly. Ramzi slipped across the room and opened the curtains. Then he sneaked back to the landing and tiptoed quietly downstairs.

When he reached the kitchen, he switched on his torch. As the circle of white light flickered around the room, he felt like a thief in the night.

Sounds of the sleeping house echoed in his ears.

"*Clunk,*" went the boiler.

"*Tick, tick, tick,*" went the clock.

21

"*Hummmm,*" went the fridge.

Ramzi tiptoed through the conservatory and turned the key in the door. Outside on the patio, night air brushed against his skin. It made him think of ghost trains and candy floss and camping trips.

"Psssssst!" A noise came out from the shadows.

Ramzi stared into the darkness. At first he couldn't see a thing. But slowly, as his eyes adjusted to the dark, the garden became visible. It looked magical under the soft moonlight; the trees were a deep indigo and snail trails flickered like tinsel across the lawn.

"Psssssst! Ramzi! Over here!" called Shaima.

"Coming – over and out," whispered Ramzi. He wasn't exactly sure why he'd said "over and out" but it felt good. Ramzi tripped across the thick, wet grass, pretending he was an explorer searching for undiscovered lands.

Suddenly Shaima appeared from the depths of the undergrowth. Her hood was knotted tightly under her chin and her pointy little spectacled face poked out. "What took you so long?" she hissed.

Ramzi giggled. "You look like a big green slug."

"I'm *camouflaged!*" snapped Shaima.

"Oh – yeh," said Ramzi. "That's what I meant. I mean, you look really good. I mean, slugs are completely camouflaged, anyway."

Shaima stuck out her bottom lip and sulked.

"Don't be like that... I've hidden some biscuits in the shed. They're chocolate ones."

"All right," said Shaima slowly. "But I do *not* look like a slug."

"Sorry," said Ramzi, shaking his head. "Come on."

Shaima dug her hands into her pockets and followed Ramzi into the shed. When they'd eaten three chocolate biscuits each, Shaima's face began to thaw. She handed Ramzi a piece of paper.

"It's the name and address of a sleepwalking specialist," she said. "I looked him up on the internet. He's really famous. Second-best in the world. And guess what?"

"What?" asked Ramzi.

"He lives just on the other side of town." Shaima looked very pleased with herself.

"Cool," said Ramzi. He folded up the paper and put it in his pocket.

"So – what shall we do now?" asked Shaima, wiping the crumbs from her cheeks.

Ramzi closed the shed door behind them and gazed up at the stars. Butterflies danced in his stomach. Ramzi always felt excited when he looked at the stars. He remembered the stories Dad told him – about the early Muslim astronomers who made clever coloured maps of the sky. Al-Battaani, Ibn Rustah, Al-Farghaani. Their names sounded grand and mysterious.

"Calling Ramzi to Planet Earth," said Shaima.

"Huh?" Ramzi turned his head.

"I *said*, 'What shall we do now?'"

"Oh. Ermmm…" Ramzi thought for a minute. "I know. Let's look for bugs while we wait."

Shaima grinned. "I *knew* you'd say that. That's why I brought *these*." She pulled two magnifying glasses out of her pocket and directed the torchlight on to the soil. Little creatures with twitching antennae fled in all directions.

"Cool," said Ramzi.

Ramzi and Shaima were so busy looking for

bugs that they didn't notice when an upstairs light cast its pale shadow across the lawn. They didn't notice when the bedroom curtains twitched. They didn't even notice when a dark figure pressed its face against the window.

But when the kitchen light lit up the garden, Ramzi switched off his torch and whispered, "Look!"

There was a shifting shadow lurking on the patio. Shaima and Ramzi waited. Suddenly Dad emerged from the darkness. He sniffed the air and looked around. Then, without warning, he lifted up his head and hurtled barefoot across the dew-drenched lawn!

Stuck up a Tree

Dad's Dream:
There was only one snow leopard left in the entire world.
As he padded across the craggy rocks, head sunk deep
on his chest, his silver coat merged with the background.
"Snap!" His ears pricked up. It was the trigger of a rifle.
A hunter was on his trail! There was only one means
of escape. With grace and speed, he bounded across the
barren savannah and leapt into the highest branches of
a tree.

Of course, Ramzi and Shaima saw things rather differently. This is what Shaima wrote in her notebook:

12.05pm: Mr Ramadan comes out of the house wearing blue-and-white stripy pyjamas.
12.07pm: He dashes across the lawn and clambers up a tree.

12.08pm: He lies down on the top branch. It wobbles a lot.

12.15pm: Mr Ramadan wakes up and screams.

"ARGHHHHHH!" cried Dad into the night. "GET ME DOWN FROM HERE!"

An angry voice bellowed from a neighbouring window. "SOME OF US ARE TRYING TO SLEEP!" The window slammed shut.

Dad clung to the upper branch of the tree as it lurched in the breeze.

"*Dad!* What *are* you doing?" called Ramzi.

Shaima staggered out of her hiding place, her knees stiff from kneeling on the damp soil. "Mr Ramadan, listen very carefully," she began. "You've been sleepwalking. Or perhaps I should say sleep-*climbing*...."

"*Dad*," interrupted Ramzi, "get down! *Now*!"

But Dad didn't move.

Now, if Mum had been there, she would have explained that Dad was terrified of heights. Lifts in shopping malls made Dad queasy. Escalators were a trial. And cliff walks, well, they were simply unthinkable. But she was *not* there. So she couldn't explain why Dad, instead of climbing down the tree, clung to the branches, closed his eyes and gritted his teeth.

A grey-haired man wearing a velvet dressing gown suddenly appeared at Ramzi's side.

"What a palaver!" he said. "Your father's normally such a sober fellow. What's he doing up a tree at this time of night?"

Ramzi's face flushed in the darkness. "He's just bird-watching, *actually*," he replied.

"Ooh – keep your hair on!" the man teased. Then he shrugged his shoulders and peered into Shaima's hood. "Well, I never!" he said. "If it isn't Shaima Stalk! I don't fancy being in your shoes when your mother finds out."

Shaima blushed.

The man walked back into the shadows, muttering to himself as he went.

Suddenly a woman's voice yelled, "Shaima! What kind of insanity has possessed you?"

A large, robed figure appeared through the darkness.

"Oh no, it's Mum!" said Shaima.

Mrs Stalk's long *jilbab* swung as she walked towards them, and a pair of sparkly slippers peeked out beneath its dark blue folds.

"What is happening?" she shouted. "And *why* are you out of bed?"

"Sorry, Mum," pleaded Shaima. "I was just observing a case of somnambulism when Mr Ramadan climbed up a tree." She looked up into the rustling leaves.

"What! Mr Ramadan? Such a respectable member of the community! Up a tree? Is he aware that my daughter is out at night, completely without parental permission – in her brother's anorak?" Mrs Stalk shook her head in despair, the tassels on her *hijab* glittering in the moonlight.

"*No*, Mrs Stalk," said Ramzi. "Dad *didn't* know Shaima was here." His voice dropped to a whisper. "Actually, we think Dad's been sleepwalking. Shaima just came to watch."

Mrs Stalk glared at her daughter. Then she tightened her headscarf and whispered, "*Astaghfirullah!*" under her breath.

"Sorry, Mum," said Shaima sheepishly.

"Yes, sorry indeed! *Anything* could have happened to you. But first, let us sort this catastrophe out." Mrs Stalk stormed into the house.

Ramzi had never heard Mrs Stalk talk before. Not in English, anyway. But now that she was here – all big and bustling – he somehow knew that Dad would be all right.

Ten minutes later Mrs Stalk had called the fire brigade, cleaned the kitchen and made Dad an appointment with his doctor. And when the firemen had carried Dad back down to safety, she made everyone take off their boots and come inside for a cup of milky, pink cardamom tea.

"That'll put feathers on our chests, Mrs Stalk!" beamed Fireman Harris.

Mrs Stalk blushed and said she didn't know much about British birds.

Ramzi and Shaima giggled, but Dad just huddled up in his blanket and stared at his trembling hands.

Later that night, when the fire engine had rumbled out of sight and the neighbours had tired of whispering on propped-up pillows, Mrs Stalk sent Ramzi and Dad to bed. Then she texted Mum.

4 mrs R
Salem. UR Boyz need U.
Not coping too well. .
Luv Frndly N'ghbour
X X X

Finally, having "tidied up all loose ends", dusted the lounge and done a spot of ironing, she dragged Shaima home by the toggles of her hood.

On Dr Slight's Couch

A boy with curly dark hair and a man with a beard stood under a big black umbrella. The rain splashed round their shoes. They were reading a brass plaque by the side of a shiny green door:

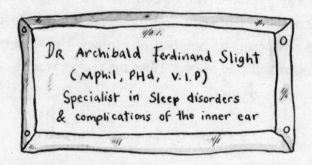

Dr Archibald Ferdinand Slight
(MPhil, PHd, V.I.P)
Specialist in Sleep disorders
& complications of the inner ear

Water dripped off the edges of their umbrella and trickled down the backs of their raincoats. The wheels of a bright red bus cut through the puddles and splashed water across the pavement.

"I'm not sure about this," said Dad. "Perhaps we should go home? Your mother will be back soon. She'll know what's best."

"Don't worry, Dad. It's OK to be scared sometimes," said Ramzi. "I mean – I'm scared of black holes."

"Me? Scared? Never!" Dad knocked on the door.

They were shown into an empty waiting room. Oil paintings hung on the walls and new books decorated the elegant coffee table. Ramzi picked one up. It was called *Ten Steps to Happiness*. Before he got past the first step, a lady in a pin-striped blouse came in. "Follow me please, Mr Ramadan," she said.

Since being rescued from the top of a tree, grey shadows had appeared under Dad's eyes. Ramzi grabbed his hand and squeezed tightly. "It's going to be OK, Dad. Honest. Just say *Bismillah*."

Dad whispered "*Bismillah*" under his breath, squeezed back and tried to smile.

They were led into a room that was even grander than the first. A tall man in a pale tweed suit stood by the large bay windows.

"Please, take off your coats and sit down, gentlemen," he said.

Ramzi looked at Dad. Dad looked at Ramzi. They took off their dripping coats and hung them on the old-fashioned stand by the door. Then they walked across the room and sank into the cushions of a luxurious burgundy sofa.

Dr Slight had a feathery yellow moustache that turned up at the corners and his eyes were a pale, sparkling blue. He winked at Ramzi.

"This is my son, Ramzi," said Dad nervously. "It was *his* idea that I came."

Ramzi stammered, "Well… it was Shaima Stalk's actually. She's like… my friend. I mean, she's a girl, but she's kind of cool… Anyway, she found out you're ranked number 2 by the… ermm… the International Sleep Disorder Foundation."

"Ah," smiled Dr Slight kindly. "Still a poor second to my great friend Professor Doubt, am I? Dear, dear…Well, it's good to meet you, Ramzi. Now, Mr Ramadan," he cleared his throat, "before we can stop your sleepwalking episodes, we must first understand their cause."

Dr Slight walked over to his desk and waved some

papers in the air. "Dr Flood sent me your notes earlier today." He muttered as he read them. "Frogs in the pantry, trips to the moon, hens in the wardrobe, snow leopards under attack...." He shook his head as he paced back and forth. Then he stopped. "Your wife is away at present, Mr Ramadan?" he asked.

Dad stroked his beard and nodded.

"But you've walked in your sleep before?"

Dad nodded again.

"You must try to talk to me, Mr Ramadan. Remember, I'm here to help."

"Go on, Dad," smiled Ramzi.

"Well," Dad began slowly, "I used to sleepwalk when I was young."

"Did you, Dad?" asked Ramzi.

"Yes, son. In fact, I wasn't much older than you. Every summer, when school finished, I was sent to help on Aunty Merzouka's farm. I worked as a shepherd. But I wasn't very good." Dad smiled. He remembered the time when he'd lost fifty sheep – they'd scattered through the fields like cotton buds and caused havoc in the market-place!

"And did you know you were sleepwalking at that time?" enquired Dr Slight.

"Oh yes – the villagers called me 'the boy with a thousand dreams'." Dad laughed quietly.

"That's totally cool!" said Ramzi.

Dad beamed.

"Go on," said Dr Slight. He took a fountain pen from his jacket pocket and scribbled something down.

"Well," sighed Dad, "I thought my sleepwalking was a thing of the past. I *thought* that 'the boy with a thousand dreams' had grown up! But I spoke to my wife on the phone this morning. She says I've been sleepwalking ever since we married!"

"Why didn't she mention it before?" asked Dr Slight.

Dad sighed. "Perhaps she's always woken me up in time?"

"Before you did anything dangerous, you mean?" Dr Slight glanced at the words *fire-engine, emergency* and *snow leopard* on the paper in his hand.

"Yes," replied Dad thoughtfully.

"And your sleepwalking has become more regular of late?"

"Yes. And much worse since Ruby's been away. Poor Ramzi has suffered."

Ramzi grinned awkwardly.

"And your work – is that suffering too?" asked Dr Slight.

"Of course. I'm so tired I can hardly walk. Falling asleep on my computer...putting salt in my coffee... I can't even wake up for *fajr* prayers!"

"I see." Dr Slight twirled his moustache. "Would you please lie down on the couch, Mr Ramadan?"

"No, thank you," said Dad.

"Dad!" exclaimed Ramzi.

"Well, are you sure it's completely necessary?" asked Dad.

"*Yes,*" said Dr Slight and Ramzi at the same time.

Dad sighed and did as he was told. Meanwhile, Dr Slight shut the curtains, popped a record on and dimmed the lights. The tinkling sound of piano music soon filled the room. Dad was lying on the couch but his body was as straight and stiff as a ruler.

Ramzi squeezed next to him. "It'll be all right, Dad," he whispered.

"Mr Ramadan," began Dr Slight in a strange, sleepy voice, "I want you to close your eyes and empty your mind. Imagine yourself in a great expanse of *nothingness*. A desert, perhaps?"

Dad closed one eye. "Why always a desert?" he muttered under his breath.

"Just do as he says, Dad," whispered Ramzi.

Dad closed the other eye.

"Now I will say a list of words," sang Dr Slight.

"He'd better not say camel," mumbled Dad.

"Ssshhhh!" said Ramzi.

Dr Slight continued in his sing-song tones. "Please answer them with the *first* word that comes into your head….Black?"

Dad stroked his beard. "Errrm. Oh. Now, let me think. The first word, you say? Errrm. The darkness of the night, perhaps?" Dad lifted his head from the cushion. "Sorry, I really don't think I can do this!"

"That's because you *think too much*, Mr Ramadan. Please try again." The piano reached a crescendo, then sank quietly into the background.

"Black?" said Dr Slight.

"Night," answered Dad.

"Happy?" said Dr Slight.

"Espresso," answered Dad.

"Home?" said Dr Slight.

"Couscous," answered Dad.

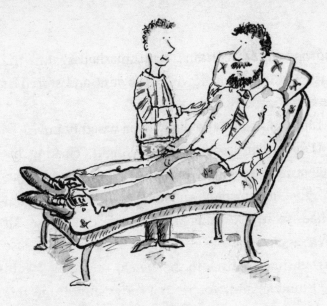

"England?" said Dr Slight.

"Grey, grey, grey," answered Dad.

"Mother?" said Dr Slight.

There was a pause.

"Sad!" answered Dad.

Suddenly Dad leapt up from the couch and knocked Ramzi to the floor. "This is *ridiculous*!" he snapped.

"*Dad!*" cried Ramzi.

"Don't worry, Ramzi," smiled Dr Slight. "The exercise has been successful and is now complete. I just need time to consider the results." Twiddling his moustache, he walked over to the bay windows and opened the curtains. Rain splashed against the glass. Dr Slight sat down at his desk and stared at his notes intently.

Dad skulked by the door like a naughty boy.

"I've got it!" exclaimed Dr Slight, clicking his fingers in the air. His pale blue eyes shone bright. "Forgive me for my rudeness, Mr Ramadan, but I had to work things out. Now do please sit down again."

Dad shuffled back to the couch.

"I understand you're not originally from this country," began Dr Slight.

"No," sighed Dad, "I'm a Berber from the mountains of Algeria."

"I see," said Dr Slight.

"Not the *desert*. The *mountains*, you understand," repeated Dad.

"Yes, of course. So sorry. My mistake." Dr Slight looked thoughtful. "It seems that we suffer from the same problem."

Dad blinked. "Really?" he said. "Do your dreams torment you too?"

"No. My dreams are under control. But I *do* suffer from nostalgia. I miss the Highlands of Scotland until my poor heart aches! They're mountains too – not desert." Dr Slight smiled kindly. "Mr Ramadan…"

"Call me Mohamed," said Dad, softening.

"Mohamed," continued Dr Slight. "Call me Archibald. May I ask you when you last went home?"

Dad sighed and tried to remember. It was *so* long ago.

"We haven't been to Algeria since I was, like, completely tiny," said Ramzi.

Dr Slight looked Ramzi up and down. He certainly wasn't tiny any more.

"Then I believe your course of action is clear." Dr Slight wafted his pen in the air and said grandly, "You are suffering from a sense of *dislocation*. Or, to put it simply, you are acutely homesick…."

Dad's face crumpled.

"There is only one thing that will ease your sleeping mind. You *must* go home."

"What? Now? Algeria? Impossible!" stammered Dad. "What about the expense? And the security problems? What of my work? And Ramzi's schooling?"

"I don't mind missing school, Dad," beamed Ramzi.

Dr Slight smiled. "You see – your son is ready to help you. As for your other questions, I'm afraid I can't answer them. I specialise in disorders of the *sleeping mind*. Disorders of the waking world are beyond my area of expertise. However, I'll write a letter to your workplace and to Ramzi's school explaining the situation."

"Cool!" said Ramzi.

But Dad was deep in thought. It was true! How his heart ached. How he *longed* for his family. How he *longed* for home!

"*Barak Allah feek*, God bless you, Archibald," said Dad at last. "I believe you are a man of great understanding."

Dr Slight smiled modestly and shook Dad warmly by the hand. Then he shook Ramzi's hand too.

Outside, on the rain-soaked pavement, Dad hugged Ramzi. "May Allah reward you, my little warrior," he said. "Now what's all this about being scared of black holes?"

"Oh, it's nothing," grinned Ramzi. "Can we go and get some sweets now?"

"What would your mother say?" laughed Dad.

Leaving Cinnamon Grove

"What? Algeria? Right *now*, love?" gasped Mum as she wheeled her suitcase into the kitchen. "But I've only just got back! Is everything all right?"

Dad didn't know where to begin. So he said, "Would you like a peppermint tea?" Then he unloaded Mum's heavy work files on to the kitchen table. "You must be tired, Ruby."

"I'm on my knees!" she sighed, dropping her suitcase by the fridge with a clunk. Then she held out her arms and smiled. "Did you miss me?"

Dad ran over and hugged Mum. "We were like two moths without our moon," he replied.

"Hmmmm," she grinned.

Dad started to chop mint leaves whilst Mum sat down. She hung her poppy-print jacket on the back of a chair and stretched her arms above her head.

"I bumped into Mrs Stalk outside," she began.

"Lovely woman. She was telling me all about the architecture in Pakistan. Fascinating. But what's all this about a fire brigade? You didn't mention *that* on the phone!"

Half an hour and two peppermint teas later, Mum was clutching Dad's hands across the kitchen table.

"Don't you worry, love," Mum said. "It's *only* money. We'll get the tickets today. We'll sell the car if we have to. I didn't like the colour anyway."

"Oh, Ruby," said Dad. "What would I do without you?"

"You'd be in a right old mess. Now, go on. Get Ramzi from school and I'll dig out those passports!"

Dad kissed Mum on both cheeks and ran out of the door.

A Flying Tortoise

"Please remove your shoes," said the lady at the airport. She was clutching a black walkie-talkie and her tummy bulged beneath her belt like a small balloon.

"Go on, Ramzi," said Mum. "Do as the lady says."

Ramzi looked at Mum with a puzzled half-smile. Then he took off his trainers and put them in a plastic tray along with his rucksack.

"What does she want my shoes for, Mum?" asked Ramzi. They were brand new with flashing lights and he didn't like to see them disappearing into the gaping mouth of an x-ray machine!

"Oh, she just needs to check they're safe," said Mum.

"Safe? Weird! I mean, they're *trainers*, Mum." Ramzi was confused.

"*Beep, beep, beep, beep,*" blurted a machine to their right. Dad had set the alarm off.

"It's all right," explained Dad cheerfully. "It's just the metal buckle on my belt." But a stern-looking security guard led him away from the queuing passengers.

"Where are they taking Dad?" asked Ramzi. He began to chew his nails.

"Oh, it's nothing, petal. They just need to ask some questions," said Mum.

When they'd picked up their hand luggage and put their shoes back on, they stood by a glass barrier and waited for Dad. Ramzi watched as two security guards checked other people's bags. They took away an old man's toothpaste and threw it in the bin! Then they asked a woman with frizzy orange hair to drink some of her baby's milk! She put the bottle to her mouth and began to suck.

Ramzi giggled. "Airports make grown-ups act completely weird, don't they, Mum?"

"They certainly do, love!"

Suddenly Mum waved a hand in the air. She'd just spotted Dad through the crowds. He was rubbing his beard and looked tired and flustered.

"Come on, Ramzi," said Mum. "I think your dad needs a coffee."

***

Later that day, a gleaming white plane coasted along the runway in France. Smartly dressed passengers were ushered through clean, empty corridors into the main terminal. Tanned men with slicked black hair and ladies in high-heeled shoes perched on stools in the airport cafes. A woman in a short red dress stroked a large pedigree dog whilst another chatted on a mobile phone, a white poodle nestled in her lap.

Ramzi stared.

"Come on, I think our check-in is over here," yelled Dad, pointing to a dusty corner of the airport. Wires hung down from the ceiling and tiles were missing from the floor.

"Ramzi! Keep up," called Mum.

Ramzi ran over to join them. There were old men in white turbans, young men in prayer caps, and tall girls in sleek headscarves with designer sunglasses perched on top. The lady in front of them wore a long stripy gown and her eyes shone with deep-black kohl. There were old women draped in silken robes and babies sparkling with gold. Ramzi felt his stomach swirl with excitement! He was going to be a real explorer at last.

Whipping a notebook and pencil out of his rucksack, Ramzi carefully drew a map of Europe and North Africa. He remembered every island and peninsula, every mountain range and shore.

"That's one of your best yet!" beamed Dad,

patting him on the shoulder. Ramzi shaded in the sea and smiled.

After a long wait, the computer screen flashed. The plane was ready for boarding. Everyone surged forward, pushing each other out of the way.

"Nothing changes!" grumbled Dad.

"Don't be so harsh," said Mum. "Look, the stewards are letting the old people and families on first. Isn't that sweet?"

"Bless you, Ruby," smiled Dad. "You always see the good in things."

Once they were on the plane, a little old woman flashed a gold-toothed smile at Ramzi. He smiled back. A white knitted shawl twisted around her shoulders and thin wisps of burgundy hair stuck out from beneath her scarf. She had star-like tattoos on her cheeks and hands – just like Nanna Ramadan's – and a big plastic bag wedged between her knees. Suddenly she leant across the aisle and spoke in soft, syrupy tones. "*Azr theen*. Look inside."

"Go on, Ramzi, have a look," said Dad.

Ramzi leant across the aisle and peered in. He saw something that looked like an army helmet. But then a little wrinkly head poked out! Ramzi jumped back and laughed. It was a tortoise!

"It's for my grand-daughter," she smiled.

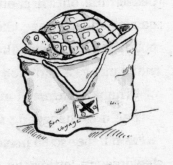

"*Cool*! Dad, can *I* have a tortoise? They live for, like, sixty years!"

"No, my little warrior. If we brought a tortoise back from Algeria, they wouldn't let us take it out of France. And there's no point having a tortoise if it has to live in France."

Ramzi sighed. He'd never understand grown-ups and their crazy rules.

It was evening when the plane landed, but the air was still warm. A little bus was waiting on the runway. It was already full of people, but a man in uniform ordered them all to squeeze in. Then it wobbled across the hot tarmac and dropped them off by some dusty glass doors.

Inside the terminal, there was a buzz of excitement. Everyone was restless, eager to see family and friends. Mum wrapped a bright turquoise scarf around her head and Dad smoothed down his beard. Ramzi didn't have a scarf or a beard so he pushed the hot curls off his face. After many more queues and baggage checks, Mum, Dad and Ramzi popped out of the smoky airport and into the bright white air.

"Thank Goodness for that!" said Mum.

Dad was struggling with the heavy cases. They were bulging with presents for family and friends. Suddenly a young man with a dark tumble of curls came running over and hugged Dad tight.

"*Salem,* big brother," he cried. He kissed Mum on both cheeks and lifted Ramzi into the air, spinning him round and round. Ramzi felt giddy and had to lean against a dusty palm tree until the world stopped spinning.

"Kader!" laughed Dad. "You've grown even taller than me!"

"It's the sun," smiled Uncle Kader. "But what about you? You're *so* pale. I hope you haven't turned into a European!"

"Arghhh," growled Dad jokingly. He pretended to punch Uncle Kader in the ribs and they hugged and kissed each other again and again.

"It's been too long, little brother," said Dad.

"Come on," grinned Uncle Kader. "Everyone's

waiting to see you. Especially you, Ramzi," he said, pinching Ramzi's cheek.

They hopped into Uncle Kader's little yellow Renault 5 and jammed the luggage into the boot. Then they showed their passports to a group of soldiers. The soldiers narrowed their eyes and stared into the car. Ramzi stared back. As they drove away from the airport, Ramzi pressed his face against the back window of the car and watched the soldiers' rifles sparkle in the sunlight.

The Town that Never Slept

They drove through empty salt marshes and bustling towns, through twisting green forests and vast yellow wheat-fields. They spotted storks nesting on the top of minarets and birds of prey soaring across the sky. Women in brightly patterned dresses herded cows along the roadside and children stood in fields, shepherding flocks of long-eared sheep.

It was just before sunset when they arrived. The town was perched on top of a rocky orange mountain and the houses were made from pale yellow stones. Behind the town stood an even taller mountain and, in the fading sunlight, you could see the dark mouths of caves where people had lived in forgotten times.

The car wound up a narrow, bumpy street and eventually came to a halt. There was a big silver water cistern at the end of the road and grape vines hung around the brightly painted metal doors.

Excited faces were peering out through upstairs shutters. Everyone was trying to catch a glimpse of the returning son!

Dad got out of the car. He took a deep breath and went inside an open door. Mum, Ramzi and Uncle Kader followed.

"*Assalemu Aleikum*! Peace be upon you!" beamed Nanna Ramadan. Her face was patterned with star-shaped tattoos and her burgundy hair shone like roasted conkers. "Come inside," she said, squeezing Dad tight. She kissed Mum  on both cheeks again and again. Then she turned to Ramzi.

"*Masha'Allah*! Praise be to God!" she exclaimed. "You look just like Mohamed when he was a boy."

Ramzi smiled and hugged her round the waist. He hadn't seen her since he was a baby, but she smelt like home: of rose-water and freshly baked bread.

Inside, the townhouse was full of people, food and

noise. Ramzi tucked into nut-filled, diamond-shaped cakes that dripped with syrup, and drank ice–cold lime juice that made his lips tingle. Cousins, aunts and uncles jostled to greet him and he was hugged and kissed until he felt giddy!

Outside, gun shots were fired into the night air. It was late, but no one wanted to leave. Shoes of every size and colour had piled up by the front door and every room in the house was brimming with smiles and laughter. When the last guests eventually went home, Mum and Dad found Ramzi curled up asleep on the stairs! With happy hearts and tired legs, they kissed his flushed cheeks and carried him up to bed.

***

It was still dark outside when a strange sound woke Ramzi. He leapt off his mattress and looked around. Dad was still asleep in the corner of the room. Ramzi listened again. The noise was coming from outside. He tiptoed across the warm tiles and opened the shutters. Night air filled the room.

"*Allaaaahu akbaaar, Aallaaaaaaahu akbaaar!*"

The deep warbling sound filled the street. A few seconds later, another call sounded. Then another. Then another. Soon, the whole town was vibrating with noise.

Mum yawned and opened her eyes. "It's just the call to prayer, Ramzi," she said.

"But it's coming from completely *everywhere!*" said Ramzi.

"We're not in England now, sweetheart," said Mum. "There are mosques all over town and they each do their own *adhan*, their own call."

"Wow!" said Ramzi. He gazed into the noisy darkness. A jasmine plant twisted along the wall beneath the window. The sweet smell reminded him of the florist shop back home.

"Is this going to happen *every* morning, Mum?" Ramzi rubbed his eyes.

"Of course it will, love. Why don't you join me for *fajr* prayer?" Mum did her ablutions and twisted a stripy blue scarf around her long curly hair. Then she spread a prayer mat on the floor. When Ramzi had finished washing his feet, he rushed to join her.

"God bless you, love," she said when they'd finished. "Now *try* and get some sleep."

But Ramzi couldn't. He just lay awake and listened. The heavy steel door of the house banged shut. It was Uncle Kader leaving for the mosque. There were footsteps outside. People were passing the house, speaking in hushed voices. Ramzi strained to listen. A dog barked. A baby cried. Water started to gurgle through the pipes, filling up the tank on the roof.

Suddenly, a man with a piercing voice shouted from beneath the window. "*F'tayr!*"

Ramzi sat up with a start.

"*F'tayr, F'tayr!*" the man yelled again.

Ramzi rushed over to Mum. "What's happening now?" he asked.

"It's nothing," said Mum sleepily. "It's just a man selling cakes. Uncle Kader might bring you some for breakfast if you're lucky. Now back to bed or you'll be too tired to play with your cousins."

But Ramzi couldn't sleep. It was getting light outside. The edges of the shutters were starting to glow. He wriggled under his sheet.

"BANG! BANG! BANG!" There was a clash of drums and the strumming of guitars.

Ramzi leapt up again. "What's *that*?" he exclaimed.

Mum got up and wandered over to the window. The edges of her long white nightdress skimmed the floor. She pushed open the shutters and a shaft of sunlight lit up the room. Ramzi poked his head outside.

"Oh!" said Mum. "It's the new bride from next door."

A young woman was leaning out of the downstairs shutters of the house opposite. Her face was thick with make-up and she had glitter in her hair. Mum waved and smiled. The new bride scowled and disappeared behind the shutters.

"Nanna warned me about her," whispered Mum. "She likes to play loud music from dawn until dusk. Her husband gave her a huge CD player as a wedding present. I bet he regrets it now! Oh well."

Mum looked at Ramzi. "I don't think we'll get back to sleep now, will we?"

"No way," sighed Ramzi, pushing the curls out of his eyes. "Shall I wake Dad?"

"No, poppet, best leave him," Mum said.

They both looked towards Dad as he snored gently in the corner of the room.

"Dr Slight was right, wasn't he, Mum? Dad just needed to come home."

"Yes, Ramzi, I think he did." Mum looked sad.

"Mum," said Ramzi. "Dad's not the same here, is he?"

"What do you mean, love?"

Ramzi tried to explain. "Well, at home, he sounds

a bit funny and looks a bit different. But here, he's kind of like everyone else."

"I know what you mean," said Mum slowly.

"*Actually*," Ramzi continued, "now *you* sound a bit funny and look a bit different."

"Me? Funny?" exclaimed Mum.

Ramzi giggled. "Well, you keep getting your sentences back to front and..."

"You cheeky little whippersnapper!" said Mum. She leapt up and chased Ramzi across the room.

"You'll wake up Dad," giggled Ramzi.

But Dad didn't wake up. Not even when Mum caught Ramzi and tickled him until he escaped and ran downstairs.

After a lovely breakfast of *f'tayr*, goat's milk and apricot jam, Ramzi put on his cap and went to play outside. Meccy and Amel – two of his cousins – were waiting by the front door.

"*Salem*," they grinned. "Hello, we brought you a lollipop."

Meccy and Amel were brother and sister – but you couldn't really tell. Meccy was short and chubby with a cheeky grin and a chipped tooth, whilst Amel was tall and graceful and reminded Ramzi of a stork.

They both started speaking at the same time and Ramzi couldn't understand a word.

"Talk slowly, please," begged Ramzi.

But Meccy and Amel spoke *so* fast – not like the slow, clear words Dad spoke at home. No one seemed to mind when Ramzi made mistakes, though, and soon he was able to keep up.

"Listen to my grandson," boasted Nanna Ramadan. "His Arabic is better than mine!"

But it was Ramzi's maps that impressed Meccy and Amel the most. They would sit and watch in delight as Ramzi scratched intricate drawings across the broken pavement in bright-green chalk.

And so the days passed. Ramzi played without a care under that clear, blue sky. He raced his cousins on their bikes, nibbled hot, buttery pancakes and splashed buckets of water to settle the dust. And whilst he raced under the sun, Mum sketched from the balcony, Nanna Ramadan made fresh bread and crunchy biscuits... and Dad?

Well, Dad slept and slept and slept!

The Thing in the Woods

One morning, while Dad still lazed in bed, Ramzi heard about *the thing that lived in the woods*. The children all called it 'Boulelli'.

"Don't drop the snail shell or Boulelli will get you," teased Amel.

Meccy threw the snail shell into the air and caught it on the back of his hand. But it wobbled and fell off.

"Doesn't matter anyway," said Meccy. "Boulelli's not real."

"*Of course* he's real," said Amel. "He eats children. *Everybody* knows that!" She arranged the tiny stones into clusters, threw a glistening white snail shell into the air, and snatched up the clusters before the snail shell landed firmly back on her hand.

Meccy's eyes had gone all watery.

"Sorry," said Amel. "Boulelli won't *really* get you. Honest."

Meccy sniffed and wiped his eyes.

"Who's 'Boulelli'?" asked Ramzi.

Meccy and Amel looked at each other in surprise. They'd never met a child who didn't know about Boulelli. *Everyone* knew about Boulelli.

"I'll tell him, I'll tell him," cried Meccy.

"No," said Amel firmly. "I'm the eldest." She leant so close to Ramzi's face that the lace on her white *hijab* tickled his nose. "It's the name of the thing in the woods," she whispered. "It means... *Father of Silk.* "

Ramzi shrugged his shoulders. He didn't understand.

"You know... what do you call it?" Amel chewed her lip. "The thing that makes the web."

"And sucks the juices out of flies," added Meccy.

"Spider!" cried Ramzi, "A spider – that eats children?"

Meccy and Amel nodded their heads.

***

Upstairs, Dad had just woken up and was peering over the balcony. "Look, Ruby," he yawned. "Ramzi's playing 'stones' with his cousins. I used to *love* playing that. I was the best."

"I bet you were," smiled Mum. She put down her pen and leaned over to look. "Oh dear, Amel's just given him *another* lollipop," she said.

"That's what he's missing in England," sighed Dad.

"Don't be silly," said Mum. "He'd have no teeth by the time he was twelve!"

"No," snapped Dad. "Not *lollipops*! I was talking about *family*. *Family*. That's what he's missing."

"Oh... yes... of course," stammered Mum. She blinked back a tear and hurried inside.

Dad scurried after her. "I'm sorry," he said quietly. "I wasn't talking about... I mean... I didn't mean... "

"I know," said Mum.

Dad took Mum's face in his hands. "Don't be sad, Beauty," he said.

"I just wish I could've given Ramzi a little brother or sister, that's all," whispered Mum.

"Ruby Ramadan," said Dad firmly. "When will you remember that you're *not* in charge of the Universe. Whatever God wills will be."

Mum smiled but she still looked sad.

Back down on the pavement, Ramzi was crunching on the remains of the lemon-sherbet lolly. It fizzed in his mouth and made his lips tingle.

Amel was still whispering in her best 'ghost-telling' voice and Meccy and Ramzi looked scared.

"But what does he look like?" asked Ramzi.

"No one's ever seen Boulelli's face," replied Amel, "but it's evil and angry and mad."

"How come no one's seen his face?"

"Ah… that's because of his long Berber cape. It has a pointed hood that covers his bloodshot eyes."

Meccy started to bite his nails.

"Go on," said Ramzi.

"People say that he carries a twisted stick that he shakes at the thundery sky."

"But he doesn't live in town, does he?" Meccy looked nervous.

"No," said Amel. "He lives up in the woods. Deep in the forest. Just at the edge of the town. Alone… in the darkness…with dead children's bones!"

"RAMZI," yelled a voice.

Ramzi leapt out of his skin! But it was just Uncle Kader, driving past in his little yellow car.

"Can we not talk about Boulelli any more, please?" said Meccy.

"Good idea," nodded Ramzi.

"OK," shrugged Amel. She passed Ramzi the stones and the snail shells. "Your turn," she said.

Ramzi threw a glistening white snail shell high into the air, but it landed on Meccy's head.

"Owwww!" cried Meccy. "You're dangerous."

"Sorry," laughed Ramzi. "It's my first time."

"What?" exclaimed Amel. "Don't you play snails in Cinnamon Grove?"

"Never."

Meccy looked shocked. "But you *must* have snails in England. *Everybody* has snails."

"Yeh, 'course," said Ramzi. "It's just we don't throw empty snail shells around."

"What do you do with them?" asked Amel.

"Nothing," said Ramzi.

"Nothing!" Meccy gasped. "I'm *so* glad I don't live in England," he said.

"Me too," agreed Amel.

"But it's really nice," insisted Ramzi.

"Don't worry," said Meccy, putting his tanned little arm around Ramzi's shoulders. "You're with us now."

Hamza's Dare

It wasn't long before Ramzi heard Boulelli's name again. He was drawing Africa on the pavement for his cousins when Mum and Dad came back from the souk.

"Algeria's *much* bigger than that!" laughed Dad as he strode past. He had a long patterned rug over his shoulder and a silver teapot in his hand.

"Look what I bought," said Mum. She swished three tangerine-and-emerald-coloured headscarves in front of their noses.

"They're lovely," sighed Amel.

"Well, in that case, this one's for you," smiled Mum. "I'll give the others to Shaima and Mrs Stalk."

"What about me and Meccy?" asked Ramzi.

"Call me old-fashioned," laughed Mum, "but you'd look a bit funny in a headscarf."

"Mum," groaned Ramzi.

"Share these instead," said Mum. She gave Meccy a bag of salted cashew nuts and Ramzi a bottle of mineral water. Then she followed Dad inside.

When the heavy metal door had banged shut, Amel looked at Ramzi and said, "What's the matter with Aunty Ruby?"

"What d'you mean?" asked Ramzi.

"Didn't you notice?" said Amel. "There's a strange rash across her nose."

"There's not," said Ramzi, puzzled.

"There is," said Meccy. "It's sort of pale brown and splotchety."

Ramzi wrinkled his eyebrows and thought hard. Suddenly he understood. "Oh! You mean her *freckles*! They *always* come out in the sunshine."

"But will she be all right?" asked Meccy.

"'Course she'll be all right! They're just *freckles*!"

Amel looked cross. "Look, Ramzi," she said. "Aunty Ruby is your Mum. You should look after her. The Prophet – peace be upon him – said: Heaven is at the feet of the Mother. *No one* is more important."

Meccy nodded seriously.

"I know," said Ramzi, trying not to laugh, "but freckles aren't dangerous. *Promise*."

Just then, a tall boy yelled at Ramzi from the end of the street. "OI, YOU!" He was lanky and looked mean and slick – all bones and t-shirt.

"Just ignore him," whispered Amel.

"YEH, YOU," he shouted again.

A group of gangly-looking boys came round the corner to join him.

"What do you want?" asked Ramzi.

The boy stared at Ramzi hard.

Ramzi felt his throat dry up. He grabbed the bottle of water by his side and had a swig.

"Look, brothers," sneered the boy. "Baby Ramadan can only drink nice clean water. *Ours* makes him sick." The boy put a finger in his mouth and pretended to vomit on the floor.

"Leave him alone, Hamza," said Meccy.

"Shut it, shorty."

Meccy started to cry.

"What's your problem?" asked Ramzi.

"*You*," said the boy. "You're our problem. Coming here with your flashy trainers and your flashy clothes, thinking you're something special. Well, you're not. You're *nothing*."

The boy kicked Ramzi's bottle of water high into the air and it jetted out in circles as it spun across the road.

"I'll tell my dad," said Amel.

"Like I care," snarled Hamza. "Just tell Baby Ramadan to go back to his *own* country. We don't want his sort round here." Without warning, Hamza pulled some bright-green chewing gum out of his mouth and threw it at Ramzi's face!

Ramzi stared at the floor, anger bubbling in his stomach.

"Go inside, Ramzi," said Amel. "Get your dad."

But Ramzi didn't move. Not an inch. You see, something like this had happened before. Back in England. It was after football practice. That's when he'd heard them. "Go back home, Bin Laden. We don't need Pakis here."

Ramzi had crumpled inside. And he'd run away. He'd run until he could hardly breathe. But he wasn't going to run away now. Not this time.

"I'm not scared of you," Ramzi said quietly.

"Wazzat?" growled Hamza.

"I said, I'm *not* scared of you." Ramzi stood up and tried to look tall.

Hamza wiped the sweat off his forehead. "Oooh – I'm shaking," he said.

But Ramzi felt so angry, he didn't care what happened. He stuck out his chin and said, "Actually, this is *my* country just as much as it's *yours*."

The group of boys sniggered like a pack of hyenas and looked at their leader to see what he'd do.

Hamza spat on the floor. "Then prove it," he growled.

"OK," said Ramzi. "I will. What do you want me to do?"

Hamza threw his head back and laughed.

Then, very slowly, he wiggled his fingers in the air.

"No!" gasped Amel. "That's not fair."

"Life's not fair," hissed Hamza.

"What? What is it?" asked Ramzi.

"They want you to visit Boulelli," said Meccy.

"Boulelli?" Ramzi's heart sank. The Spider that lived in the woods? The Spider that was mean and angry and mad? The Spider that ate children?

"Tomorrow night," said Hamza. "After *Maghreb* prayers. Bring me his stick. I'll be waiting for you...."

Out of Puff

It was sunset at the edge of town. The silhouette of the woods stood out like a black cardboard cut-out against the crimson sky.

"Now, remember," said Amel, patting Ramzi on the back, "just grab Boulelli's stick and run. *Don't* get caught!"

Ramzi nodded. He was too out of breath to talk.

"*Please* let us come with you," said Meccy. "You sound all wheezy."

"It's just the hill," panted Ramzi. "Don't worry – I've got *this*." He took his inhaler out of his pocket and sucked hard. It made him feel dizzy and brave.

Ramzi's inhaler

Meccy looked impressed.

"What if someone notices you're gone?" asked Amel.

"They won't. I'll be home before they get back from the mosque," said Ramzi.

"*Insha'Allah!*" said Amel. "May Allah protect you!"

Meccy and Amel kissed him on both cheeks and scrambled back down the hill.

Suddenly, Ramzi felt alone – a tiny dot beneath the vast, star-strewn sky. He traced the twinkling pattern of the Plough with his finger – just like he did when he was at home, looking at the stars from his bedroom window.

Home. It seemed so far away. How he wished he was in his own room, back in Cinnamon Grove. Not stuck up on a mountain in the darkness. But then he remembered Dad. And the hen. And the fire brigade. And Dr Slight. And *then* he remembered Hamza and the bullies.

No. Cinnamon Grove would have to wait. Ramzi took a deep breath, said, "*Bismillah!*" and disappeared into the forest.

***

The trees grew so close together that Ramzi had to crawl on his hands and knees. Pine needles scratched his skin and hard earth made his knees sore. But he wasn't going to give up. Not now. He was going to get Boulelli's stick. *That* would show them.

Suddenly the trees stopped and Ramzi fell on to the floor with a THUD. Right in front of him, on the other side of the clearing, was an old rectangular house. The faint light coming from a tiny square window made its sharp edges just visible in the darkness.

Trembling, Ramzi crept across the clearing and hid behind the cold concrete wall. But how would he find the Spider's stick? He tried to think of a plan but he couldn't. The door was shut and the window was too high. So he just waited. Waited and listened until... *CREEeeeak*. The door opened.

Ramzi crouched in the shadows. And that's when he saw him: Boulelli. He was just like Amel had said. He wore a long, dark Berber cape and a hood that hung over his face.

Ramzi closed his eyes and prayed that Boulelli wouldn't see him. "Please, Allah, make me invisible," he said again and again in his head.

When he opened his eyes, the figure had gone. Gone into the woods. Ramzi took a deep breath. This was his chance. Without thinking, he crept out of the shadows and pushed open the creaking door. His eyes scanned the dimly lit room. A bed... a curtain...a fireplace... a stick! There, resting against the wall.

Ramzi rushed over, grabbed it and ran for the door. But the candlelight was weak and Ramzi couldn't see. He tripped on something. "Arghh!" he yelled as he crashed to the ground.

"*Eshkun*? Who is it?" called a voice.

Ramzi leapt to his feet and stumbled out of the door, leaving the stick behind. It was Boulelli! Boulelli the child-eater! He was coming to get him! Ramzi ran across the clearing until he reached the trees. Then he dived into the darkness of the forest.

When he was sure that he was safe, Ramzi stopped. Puffing and out of breath, his whole body shook. But he'd done it! He'd been into Boulelli's house and escaped alive! He didn't care what Hamza said about the stick. He wasn't going back. No way.

He carried on crawling through the forest – among the needles and the dust – but his chest began to hurt. It felt tight and sore – as if wasps had stung him on the inside. He reached for his inhaler but it wasn't in his pocket! He tried the other pocket… no… it had gone.

Hurriedly, Ramzi began to retrace his steps. It *must* have fallen out in the forest. He fumbled on the ground in the darkness. Nothing. Just needles and dust. As he got closer and closer to the clearing, a lump of panic swirled in the pit of his stomach. Perhaps it was in Boulelli's house? He remembered falling over. What if? Oh no.

He didn't want to go back inside the Spider's trap. He didn't want to become a pile of bones. But his chest was getting tighter and tighter. He could hardly breathe….There was no choice. Ramzi stumbled into the clearing.

The Spider's Prophecy

By the half light of the moon, a hooded figure found a boy lying on the ground. Boulelli dragged him to his feet and, with great effort, carried him inside.

"This is it!" thought Ramzi. "He's going to eat me!"

Boulelli dropped him on to something soft. Ramzi struggled for breath. He wanted Mum and Dad. He wanted Cinnamon Grove. He wanted to be at home.

Something cold hit against his teeth. A puff of cold air filled his mouth.

Ramzi sucked in deeply. Slowly, his chest started to open. The Spider had given him his inhaler! He could breathe again! He opened his eyes and looked around the room. The hooded figure was huddled over the fire... The Spider was smaller than Ramzi had imagined.... He thought about running but he felt too weak.

Suddenly the Spider turned round.

Ramzi gasped.

"I'm not going to hurt you," Boulleli said.

"But...but..." stammered Ramzi.

Boulelli smiled.

"But... but... you're not a man!" cried Ramzi.

"No, I'm not," laughed the Spider as she pulled back her hood. Long tresses of hair fell about her face, and her eyes smiled kindly in the candlelight.

Ramzi had never seen anyone so completely and utterly beautiful. "But I thought..." stuttered Ramzi.

"Everybody does," said the girl. "Please don't tell anyone I'm not."

"But why...?"

"It's a long story," sighed the girl.

Ramzi waited, but she said nothing.

"So if you aren't Boulelli, then who are you?" he asked.

"My name is *Scheherazade*. But shouldn't I be the one asking the questions? After all, weren't you trying to steal my stick?"

"I'm sorry," said Ramzi. "It's just that... well... Hamza and his gang dared me."

"What? *Those* bullies," said Scheherazade. She seemed to know them. Her face tightened with anger. "They made my dad's life miserable."

"Your dad?" asked Ramzi, confused.

"Yeh – they called him *Boulelli*."

"But I thought Boulelli was mad. I thought he hunted children?"

Scheherazade huffed and stared into the fire. "No. *Children* hunted Boulelli," she said. "Hamza and his horrible friends used to throw stones at him. Can you believe that? Dad just waved his stick to try to scare them away."

Ramzi suddenly felt ashamed of himself.

"That's awful," he said. "I'm really sorry. I didn't know."

"That's OK," smiled Scheherazade.

While they were talking, a lovely, sleepy smell

filled the room. Scheherazade took an old kettle that hung above the fire and poured out two cups of a dark, steaming, green liquid.

"Have some tisane," she said. "It will help your chest."

Ramzi took a deep sip. It tasted of all the wonderful things he couldn't name.

"Why were they so mean to your dad?" he asked.

"He was *different*, I s'pose. People didn't understand him. That's why he moved up here."

"And you came with him?" asked Ramzi.

"No. Not at first. I stayed with an aunt in town. But then Dad got sick. I couldn't bear for him to be alone. And now he's gone. Well…" She paused. "I like it here."

"Where's he gone?" asked Ramzi.

Scheherazade looked upwards.

"Oh! Sorry!" blurted out Ramzi.

Scheherazade said nothing.

The silence filled with questions. There was so much Ramzi wanted to know. Why was a beautiful girl living all alone? And why did she pretend to be Boulelli? And why did people say Boulelli was mad?

"What was so different about your dad?" he said at last.

Scheherazade sighed. "I think it was the war. I think it damaged him inside. You know... when the French were here. Whenever he heard planes, he thought the bombs were coming again. It made him act strange. And, well, he thought..." She blushed. "He thought he had a special gift: that he knew the secrets of the future." Tears began to flow from her eyes. "I wish he was still here," she cried.

Ramzi didn't know what to say. He just wanted to make her feel better. The words came out of his mouth before he had time to think

"My dad acts weird too," he said.

Scheherazade looked surprised. "What does he do?" she asked.

"He sleepwalks. Climbs trees in his pyjamas. That sort of thing."

Scheherazade raised her eyebrows and smiled.

"It's not that bad," said Ramzi. "He doesn't think there's a war still on or anything. And children don't throw stones at him. But it does make him really unhappy. And he doesn't want to go back. To England, I mean."

"Hang on a minute!" exclaimed Scheherazade. She plonked her tisane on the floor, jumped up and disappeared behind an old grey curtain that divided the room. Ramzi could hear the rustling of paper. Then Scheherazade flung open the curtain – a big, brown leather book in her hands.

"What are you doing?" asked Ramzi.

"My dad! My dad!" she cried excitedly. "He *wasn't* mad! He *could* tell the future. He *told* me you were going to come. It's all written here!"

"What?" exclaimed Ramzi.

"Look," said Scheherazade, pointing to a fading yellow page.

My dearest daughter,

Though I cannot forget the past, nor can I empty my mind of the future. One day a boy will come to you. He will try to steal. But do not be afraid. In a time to come, he will be a source of great happiness. But first, you must tell him this:

Only he can save his father from his nightmares.

For it has been written and will come to pass.

Scheherazade shut the book with a SNAP.

"He meant *you*," she said.

Ramzi was lost for words. He didn't know what to think. "I better go," he said at last. "They'll be asking where I am."

"Of course," grinned Scheherazade. She looked happy. "Just don't tell anyone about me. And here – take my stick! I don't need it any more."

Ramzi smiled and stood up. "Thanks. And thanks for the tisane. And for – well – you know. But will I see you again?"

"Oh yes," said Scheherazade. "Of that I'm sure."

Sugar in the Soup

When Ramzi got back to town, Hamza was waiting.

"Here's your stupid old stick," said Ramzi. He wasn't scared of Hamza any more. He brushed him aside and walked into Nanna Ramadan's house.

Hamza looked puzzled and surprised.

"Where have you been?" asked Mum. She looked worried.

"Sorry, Mum, I dropped my inhaler. I had to go back and find it."

"Well, you should have told us where you were going," said Mum.

"I said he'd be all right," grinned Dad. "Young boys need a bit of adventure!"

Meccy and Amel were in the lounge playing games on Nanna's mobile phone.

"*Alhamdulillah*! Thanks be to God! You're alive!" they shouted when they saw that their cousin was safe.

Ramzi winked.

"What a strange thing to say!" said Nanna Ramadan. "Now, give your Nanna a kiss. I've made you all some of my special crunchy biscuits. Come on."

They all kissed Nanna on the head and helped her up and into the kitchen.

"Did you do it? Did you see Boulelli? Did you get the stick?" whispered Meccy excitedly, biscuit crumbs shooting out of his mouth.

Ramzi nodded – his cheeks too full of sugar and crunch to speak.

"You are amazing," sighed Amel.

***

That summer, Ramzi didn't see the Spider – or Scheherazade – again. But he thought about her often. And he remembered what she'd said: *only he could save his father from his nightmares*. But how? That was the question. Or maybe it didn't matter any more? After all, Dad seemed so much better now. It was Ramzi and Mum who were beginning to struggle.

You see, in the town on top of the hill, the wedding season had begun. Parties echoed off the mountains and the banging of drums and whistle of pipes filled the streets. Rifles were fired into the air amid the dancing, and women *ululated* from the windows. And just when the noises of the night had quietened down, the call to prayer began. Ramzi, Mum and the town on the hill top never really slept!

But Dad did. The shadows disappeared from under his eyes and the bounce came back in his step. Every morning, he raced down the staircase for breakfast. Every morning, Ramzi and Mum rubbed their eyes and stumbled along behind.

"My son," said Nanna. "You've not changed! You're still my young lion that stretches on top of the mountain."

Dad leant over and kissed Nanna on the forehead.

"*Subhan'Allah!* God is glorious!" she said as she looked into his mouth. "And you've still got all your own teeth!"

Dad laughed.

But Nanna looked thoughtful. "How much longer will Ramzi and my bride be with us?" she asked.

Nanna always called Mum 'my bride'.

Dad held Nanna's star-patterned hand in his. "We'll have to return to England soon, *Yemma*," he said sadly.

Nanna looked away.

The next time Nanna spoke, her voice was cold and hard. "Here, Ramzi, eat these," she said. She passed Ramzi some dates. "Just look at your bony knees – The English don't feed you properly!"

"OK, Nanna," said Ramzi. He looked at his knees – they were a *bit* bony. Perhaps she was right? He kissed her conker-coloured hair and ate as many dates as he could.

"Now take me outside, Mohamed," Nanna ordered. She waved her hand towards the door.

Dad picked up a cushion and helped Nanna to her favourite spot, from where she always watched the passers-by.

Ramzi was playing with some children in the street. *Everybody* wanted to be his friend. They had all heard about how he'd stood up to Hamza. And about how he'd escaped from the Spider.

"Tell us about it? What did he look like?" whispered the children.

But Ramzi just shook his head and yawned.

Meanwhile, Dad tried to speak to Nanna. But she folded her arms and looked the other way. Eventually, Dad gave up and headed back inside.

"Oh, this is *awful*!" cried Mum. She was in the kitchen, stirring a great big saucepan. Wisps of pale-brown hair clung to her hot face.

"It'll be fine, whatever it is," said Dad quietly.

"Don't be silly," snapped Mum. "It *won't* be fine. Last time I cooked, I gave your brothers food poisoning!" She burst into tears. "Sorry – it's just that it's all so different here. I don't even know what most of these things are." She pointed to a shelf covered with bags full of brightly coloured spices. "And I think I've just put sugar in the soup!"

Dad smiled and tasted a spoonful. "Not enough salt, that's all," he said gently.

"Will you take over, please?" begged Mum.

***

It was getting hotter outside. Ramzi hadn't slept properly for ages and his legs were beginning to ache. He came in to shelter from the sun. But it was hot everywhere. Even inside.

"Cinnamon Grove's *never* too hot," thought Ramzi. "And I bet Shaima's not all hot and sweaty. I want to go home."

He wanted to be on his own. So he dragged his dusty feet across the marble floor and slumped on to the hard stone stairs. Grumbling to himself, he watched Dad in the kitchen. Dad was a brilliant cook. He added a dash of one herb and a pinch of another to Mum's soup, and soon delicious smells filled the house. Not that Ramzi cared. He wasn't hungry. But Mum smiled with relief and gave Dad a hug.

Dad looked thoughtful.

"What's the matter, Mohamed?" asked Mum.

"I was just thinking... we'll have to go back to England soon."

"That's all right," said Mum. "The sleepwalking has stopped now."

"But that's just because we're here," said Dad. "It'll come back in England."

Mum forced a smile. "Of course it won't, love."

But she didn't look sure.

They both fell silent and listened to the pan bubble. Ramzi didn't move.

"I suppose we could stay here?" suggested Dad.

"What? Forever?" Mum gulped.

"Why not?" said Dad. "Ramzi's happy here."

"I think the soup's burning!" said Mum.

Ramzi ran upstairs and slammed the door.

A Sheep in the Kitchen

"Argghhh!" screamed Ramzi. He dropped his empty cup on to the hard floor.

"What is it?" yelled Mum. She'd just woken up and was still in her nightdress.

"Mum – I think I'm *sleepwalking*..." stammered Ramzi. "It's just that... it's just that I *think* I can see a sheep in the kitchen!"

"What?" shrieked Mum. She ran down the stairs to join him.

"Look!" said Ramzi.

Mum peered through the hatch. "You're not sleepwalking, petal," she said slowly. "There *is* a sheep in the kitchen."

"Oh!" exclaimed Ramzi.

"*Baaaaaaaaaaa,*" said the sheep.

Just then, Dad bounded up behind them.

"Aha!" he said. "You've found her. Isn't she beautiful? We got her from the market just before sunrise."

"But why's *a sheep* in the kitchen, Dad?" asked Ramzi.

"This is where we'll keep her 'till the party," beamed Dad.

"What party?" asked Mum.

"Uncle Kader and Nanna have arranged one to celebrate our homecoming. Everybody's coming!" Dad was brimming with excitement.

"But why is a *sheep* coming to the party?" asked Ramzi cautiously.

"Well," said Dad, "the guests will need to be fed."

"You mean…" stuttered Ramzi.

"Oh!" gasped Mum.

"*BAaaaaaaaaaaaaaa!*" said the sheep.

95

**

The party was a great success. There was dancing and singing, and the food was delicious.

But when everyone left, Ramzi and Mum looked glum.

"Come on, you two!" said Dad. "Cheer up!"

"We're just a bit tired, love," answered Mum.

"Huh," grunted Ramzi. He was staring at the remains of the lamb couscous.

"It's better than buying it from a supermarket," said Dad. "We thanked Allah *and* we made sure the sheep was treated kindly."

"Huh," grunted Ramzi again.

"It just takes a bit of getting used to, that's all," said Mum. "Besides, we're so tired." Mum yawned but Dad's face clouded over.

"*You* don't want to stay here, do you, Ruby?" he said.

"It's not that, love, it's just that…"

"It *is* that!" shouted Ramzi. "*I want to go home!*" He jumped up and ran out of the door.

Dad's sun-tanned cheeks went suddenly grey.

"Take no notice!" said Mum. "There's been too

much excitement. We'll all feel better after a good night's sleep!"

But that night, no one could rest.

Under the Stars

As the long days passed, the air grew hotter and hotter. Soon Ramzi couldn't play in the street. When he tried, the sun nearly knocked him to the ground. Besides, there was no point – the whole town went to sleep after lunch, even the children. Ramzi tried to sleep too but he couldn't. So he just listened to the whirring of the fan as it blew stale air around the room. Sweat gathered behind his knees and his throat became dry.

But Dad looked more boyish every day. After one hot, stuffy siesta, Dad jumped up from his mattress, his eyes bright and wide.

"Come on, Ramzi," he said. "Why don't you join me and my friends for a game of cards?"

Ramzi groaned. He was hot and tired and didn't want to move.

"Go on," said Mum. "It'll do you good." So, with hands dug deep in his pockets, Ramzi went.

Outside, the day was beginning to cool. There was even a slight breeze in the air. Shops were lifting their shutters and cafés were opening their doors.

Ramzi began to feel better as he walked with Dad through the narrow streets of the town.

At last, they came to a huge, bustling café. It was full of men in white gowns huddled around metal tables. Some were puffing smoke out of a long pipe and others were chewing pistachio nuts.

"Over here, stranger!" called a man with an enormous moustache.

"Mustafa!" shouted Dad. He pulled Ramzi's arm and they squeezed through the tables towards a group of smiling men.

The men stood up and took it in turns to hug Dad. "Where have you been hiding?" they said. "We thought you'd forgotten us."

"How could I?" said Dad. There were tears in his eyes.

"And this must be your son!" said a man with a big straw hat.

Dad grinned.

The men ruffled Ramzi's curls and kissed his cheeks.

"*Assalemu Aleikum*," said Ramzi.

"*Subhan'Allah!*" cried the man with the moustache. "He can even speak Arabic!"

"Of course he can!" laughed Mustafa. "He's a Ramadan, through and through. Just look at that hair!"

Ramzi smiled.

A waiter brought a tray full of food and drink to the table. "Welcome back, Mohamed! It's on the house," he said.

Dad's friends sprinkled peanuts on top of their steaming mint teas while Ramzi gulped down a glass of fizzing lemonade. Then the card game began.

That evening, Dad remembered old times and laughed until his sides ached.

Ramzi had never seen his Dad giggle so much – he seemed so happy, so alive.

"This is the best place to be!" thought Ramzi. "By my dad's side."

Later that night, as they walked home through the empty streets, Dad said. "I need to talk to you, son."

"Sure, Dad," answered Ramzi. Dad sounded serious.

"You know that everyone here loves you, don't you?" said Dad.

"Yeh!" Ramzi blushed in the darkness.

"Well." Dad paused. "How would you feel about staying here? Just for a year or two?"

Ramzi looked up at the stars. Suddenly, he felt so small.

"What is it, son?" asked Dad sadly.

"I *do* completely love it here, Dad," Ramzi began, "and I'll really miss everyone when we go home. But…"

"But… this isn't your home, is it?" sighed Dad. He looked like a broken man.

"Sorry, Dad," said Ramzi. He felt awful. He remembered his dad at the card game – giggling and swigging mint tea. Ramzi hugged Dad tightly.

Dad hugged him back.

"No, of course it's not. No man can have his heart in two places! I know that better than most!" Dad sounded very far away.

"But I want to come back *every single* year, Dad. Honest."

"Do you, son?" Dad brightened.

"And I *don't* want you to start sleepwalking again, Dad. Not ever."

"No. Nor do I." Dad looked thoughtful. "Don't worry, little warrior. We'll think of something," he said.

'I *have* to think of something,' thought Ramzi. Suddenly, he remembered Boulelli's book. How could he have forgotten? But what could he do? His mind was blank.

So together, each alone with their own thoughts, father and son walked through the darkness and back to the house.

A Trip to see the Wise-Man

Dad spent the following morning in the mountains. When he got back, he was twitching with excitement.

"I've just seen Aunty Merzouka," he said, "and she's given me an idea."

Mum and Ramzi listened as Dad began. "There's a man in the countryside who cures people if they're bewitched."

Mum's eyebrows shot up into the air.

"Are you bewitched, Dad?" asked Ramzi.

Dad smiled. "No, but listen. There was a man from a nearby village who was so bewitched by a woman's beauty that he followed her day and night for a whole year! He forgot to harvest his fields, he lost all of his flock, and he wasted all of his money. He just followed her wherever she went! Now, this wise-man *cured* him. I think I should visit him too."

"So who's bewitched you?" teased Mum.

"This is serious, Ruby!" snapped Dad. "He might be able to stop my sleepwalking for good. Otherwise, I *won't* go back to England." Dad folded his arms and looked grim.

"Goodness!" exclaimed Mum.

"Let's go," said Ramzi.

****

Mum and Dad had a siesta but Ramzi couldn't rest. Thoughts kept whizzing through his mind. '*Maybe Boulelli was wrong... Maybe he was mad... Maybe the wise-man will cure Dad, not me.*'

Later that day, they set off into the hills in Uncle Kader's little yellow car. The sky was dotted with black-and-white storks, their huge, heavy wings carving great paths through the sky. They drove through bustling street markets with stalls full of olives, fresh watermelons and dates. They passed through villages where old men stared and women jostled for gold.

It was beginning to cool down when the car turned off the bumpy road and on to a dusty dirt track.

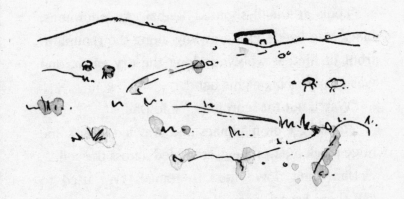

The landscape was bare. There were no trees up here. Just empty wheatfields speckled with white rocks.

In the distance, there was a little stone house breaking the blue horizon. As they drove closer, Ramzi noticed that it had a tiny door but no windows. Outside, on the dusty ground, was an old piece of wood that rested on three large stones. The car came to a halt.

"Is this it?" asked Mum.

But Dad was already out of the car. "Isn't it beautiful?" he sighed as he gazed across the fields.

Mum stood with him and held his hand. "Is this where you were born?" she asked.

Dad nodded and took a deep breath while Uncle Kader wandered off to look for a well.

"Look at this!" shouted Ramzi. An enormous, black stag beetle was crawling along the ground in front of him. It wobbled along the dry earth, and was nearly as big as his hand.

"Watch out for scorpions," said Dad.

Ramzi got on his knees and crawled after some huge black ants as they scrambled across the soil.

Dad knelt down next to Ramzi. "We used to call them French ants," he said mischievously. "Be careful though, they bite."

"AHEM!" The noise made them all turn around.

In the door of the windowless house stood a tall, slim man, with sharp cheekbones and a curious smile.

Some of his front teeth were missing but his eyes glistened. His long white gown touched the dusty floor and his turban curled round his head like a big white cat.

"*Assalemu aleikum,*" he said. His voice was soft and deep. He beckoned them to enter. They followed.

Inside, the room was empty

apart from an espresso maker, a rug, a prayer mat and a tiny gas stove. The wise-man asked them to sit on the brightly patterned rug while he sat cross-legged on the dusty earth. He clutched his bare feet in his hands and spoke in the same deep, syrupy language as Nanna.

Dad told him about England and his dreams.

"Open your heart, Mohamed Ramadan, for God has no shame of the truth," said the wise-man.

So Dad told him about Dr Slight, the hen in the wardrobe, the frogs in the pantry, the boat trip to the moon, the snow leopard and even the fire brigade.

The wise-man shook his head as he chewed on a piece of wheat. "History has no mercy," he said. "Your country haunts you and it was right you returned to your land. For it is only here that you can banish your demons!"

The wise-man started to scratch shapes into the earth with a twig. Then he closed his eyes and fell silent.

"What's he doing?" asked Mum.

"He's thinking, Mum," explained Ramzi.

They waited.

After a few minutes, the wise-man's eyes suddenly

flicked open. Slowly, he lifted three soil-stained fingers into the air. "There are three things you must do before you return to foreign shores," he said. "At first light tomorrow, you must travel to the depths of the Sahara. Find The City of a Thousand Domes. Drive east and find a tribe of Tuareg. They will bury you in hot desert sand. This will cleanse your body of dark thoughts.

"When you return, you must be wrapped in a cloth, drenched in powerful herbs, that will seep into the pores of your skin. A woman in your town will help you. Her name is Chelti Gamra. But remember this: do *not* remove the cloth until dawn! Whilst it is drawing out the nightmares, burn a snake's skin outside your front door. Do as I say and all evil spirits and mischievous djinns will be banished from your body and mind!" He rubbed the black hair beneath his turban and lay down to rest on the bare ground.

In a hushed voice, Dad explained what the wise-man had said.

"Blimey!" exclaimed Mum.

"*Cool!*" said Ramzi.

"Should we pay him?" asked Mum.

"He just wants me to say a prayer for him at the mosque," replied Dad.

"Is that all?" asked Mum. "Give him some money, love. He's got nothing."

"No. He'll be offended," said Dad. "But I think I know what he'd like." Dad took off his shoes and left them on the rickety wooden bench in front of the house.

Uncle Kader was waiting in the car. They all got in and Uncle Kader started the engine. Dust swirled around the back wheels and followed them like a sandstorm as they disappeared over the blank horizon.

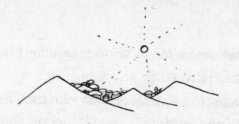

The City of a Thousand Domes

It was two days before they reached The City of a Thousand Domes. It bordered the Sahara Desert like a froth of bubbles at the edge of a sandy shore. Every house, every mosque, every shop had a perfectly curved roof.

"This is like something out of a story book!" enthused Mum, as she snapped away on her camera.

They drove up and down the busy streets until finally they found a hotel. It was the colour of sand and had a bright blue roof topped with six little domes.

"*Alhamdulillah*," said Dad. "This should do for the night."

They parked their yellow car at the back of the hotel and asked for a room. A man in a gold-trimmed robe welcomed them, and carried their bags down a cool white corridor.

"Wow!" cried Ramzi. "This is brilliant!" He didn't mind that it was hot any more. Not now he was being an explorer! A proper one who travelled to the Sahara. Just wait till his friends heard about this!

The room in the hotel was like the inside of a cave. Its walls and ceilings were white and curved. Brightly patterned cushions were strewn along the floor and carved metal lanterns dangled from the ceiling. A low wooden table sat in the middle of the room, on top of which was some cold water and a bowl of fresh fruit. Dad gave Ramzi a big slice of water melon.

"This tastes fantastic!" slurped Ramzi. Juice dribbled down his chin.

Dad carried some out to Mum, who was busy sketching on the balcony. Ramzi went to join them.

"What do you think of this, Ramzi?" asked Mum.

The town spread out in front of them like a beautiful painting. Blue, orange and golden domes curved their way into the distance.

"It's *totally cool*! But where's the desert?" asked Ramzi.

Dad lifted Ramzi up. "Over there," he said.

Just behind the furthest dome, shimmering in the sunlight, Ramzi could see the tip of a single dune. "Can we go right *now*?" asked Ramzi.

"Tomorrow," smiled Dad.

They walked to the market place and shared a huge pizza and some fizzy drinks by a fountain. Young men without helmets whizzed past on their motorbikes whilst families walked through arches, arm in arm. But as darkness fell, the Ramadans returned to their hotel. Sitting on the balcony, they listened to the sound of crickets and the soft rumble of cars.

"Does anyone live in the desert, Dad, or is it empty?" asked Ramzi.

"Of course people live there – haven't I told you about the Bedouins and the Tuaregs?" asked Dad.

"Tell us about them now, love," said Mum.

So Dad began. He told stories of men in blue turbans with black skin and sparkling blue eyes. He told them about bonfires crackling in the darkness and camel races at dawn. Then he told them about his childhood. About the Uncle who could carry a donkey on his back. About his cousins dancing with him naked in the storm. About the time when everyone called him 'the boy with a thousand dreams'.

And for the first time, they really understood. This was where Dad belonged!

That night, as they stared out at the City of a Thousand Domes, they were all too excited to sleep. So they huddled together under the twinkling stars and listened to Dad's stories until sunrise.

But what of the Spider's prophecy? Well, far away from the mountains – amongst the domes and the desert – it had faded like a long-forgotten dream. And Ramzi had only one thought: the wise-man would cure Dad now.

Buried in the Desert

"Are you *sure* you're all right, love?" said Mum.
Dad's head was sitting on top of the desert sand like
a football on the
beach! His body was
buried somewhere
beneath.

"I'm fine!" He
smiled bravely.

Mum reached into
her bag for a bottle
of sun-cream. "Well,

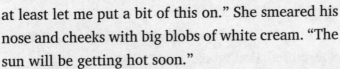

at least let me put a bit of this on." She smeared his
nose and cheeks with big blobs of white cream. "The
sun will be getting hot soon."

"That's enough," blushed Dad. "Look! I'm at the
mercy of my wife today!" he shouted to a nearby
Tuareg.

The Tuareg laughed. He was flattening sand around another man's head only feet away.

When the Tuareg stood up to his full height, Ramzi gazed spellbound. He was tall, with deep-black skin and sparkling blue eyes, just like the ones in Dad's stories. His bright blue robe stood out against the unending background of yellow sand dunes and empty turquoise sky. Ramzi had never seen anyone look so magnificent.

"Are we going to just leave you here, love?" Mum asked Dad's head.

"Not all day, Ruby! I'd die from the heat!" said Dad.

"Oh!" gasped Mum.

"Just go and sit in the shade," said Dad.

Mum looked behind her. There was a tumble-down shelter made of palm leaves and branches, nestled into a dune. Another family were sipping mint tea under its cover.

"But you've got sand in your beard," fussed Mum. She patted Dad's beard and put a sun cap on his head.

Dad blushed again.

"Come on, Mum," said Ramzi. "Leave Dad alone."

Dad winked up at his son. Ramzi winked back. Then he yanked Mum's arm and they walked towards the shade.

That day, as the white glaring sun rose in the sky, the sand grew hotter and hotter! The other man was soon dug out. He dusted himself down and left with his family. But Mum and Ramzi waited. And waited.

At last, they heard a distant voice croak, "Get me out of here!"

It was Dad.

The Tuareg picked up his robes and ran across the burning sand. Ramzi and Mum raced after him and they dug Dad out as fast as they could.

***

"Arghhh!" groaned Dad. He was slumped in the back seat of the car, his eyes closed. His beard and hair were full of sand and he looked like a shipwrecked sailor.

"Is Dad all right?" asked Ramzi.

But Mum was busy looking at the map.

"Mum," exclaimed Ramzi. "It's upside-down!"

"Have a little faith, petal. Everything's under control. I just need to find that City of a Thousand Domes!"

Ramzi grabbed the map. "You've lost us, haven't you, Mum?"

"No, of course not!" said Mum, pushing her slipping headscarf back off her forehead.

"Arghhh," groaned Dad again.

A huge oil tanker thundered past. Mum gripped the steering wheel tight.

"What does *that* mean?" asked Ramzi. He was pointing to a red triangular sign at the side of the road. It showed a little black car disappearing into a sand dune.

"Nothing, poppet," said Mum.

"Does it mean that sand dunes might swallow up the car?" asked Ramzi nervously.

"Only if we stop," said Mum.

"Blimey!" gulped Ramzi.

"Arghhh," groaned Dad.

"Look," said Mum, pointing at the horizon.

Ramzi looked. A Bedouin and his young daughter were leading five camels along the top of a distant dune.

Mum pulled over to the side of the road and scrabbled in her bag for her camera. "No wonder they're called *ships of the desert*," she sighed.

"And look over there!" shouted Ramzi. He was pointing to a cluster of palm trees. Barely visible, just peeking out from behind their deep green leaves, was a sparkling white roof. At last, they'd found The City of a Thousand Domes!

Ramzi sighed with relief.

"I told you we weren't lost," smiled Mum.

Back at the hotel, Mum and Ramzi helped Dad stumble into the shower. Dad washed the sand out of his ears and toes and scrubbed the grains out of his beard. Then he put on a white dressing-gown and drank seven glasses of ice-cold water.

"Well done, Dad, you were completely brilliant today!" Ramzi said.

Dad smiled. "Thanks, little warrior."

But Mum was looking red-faced and sad.

"What up, Ruby?" asked Dad.

"*What's up?* I'm tired. I'm covered in sand. I'm sticky. I'm hot. My husband's just been buried. And I nearly lost my family in the desert," snapped Mum. There was a pause. "Mohamed, *I want to go home,*" she said.

"Back to the damp grey skies of England?" Dad teased.

"There's nothing wrong with damp grey skies," said Mum. "Besides, I want a proper cup of tea and some fish and chips." Her voice was wobbly.

Dad smiled at Ramzi. "If we're not careful, your mother will be sleepwalking soon."

Ramzi tried to smile but he was missing home too.

Mum blinked back her tears as Dad put his arms around her waist. "Don't worry, love, you're doing really well," said Dad. "The heat of the desert drives some people mad. Why don't you and Ramzi have a shower? They've got plenty of hot water here."

"Really?" Mum brightened.

"Yes, but I'm afraid there's no cold." Dad grinned. "It's a desert problem!"

Mum laughed and bashed Dad on the shoulder. Ramzi wiped the dust from his face.

***

When they'd all freshened up and eaten some freshly picked oranges, Ramzi remembered what the wise-man had said. Something about herbs and djinns. "Dad – do you have to be wrapped up in smelly stuff when we get back?"

"That's right, Ramzi," nodded Dad.

"You won't be smelling sweet for long, then!" Mum smiled. "We'd better make the most of it."

Dad pulled the crisp, white towel from his head and threw it at Mum. She threw hers back. Ramzi picked up a cushion and launched it at Dad. Soon the hotel room was filled with flying cushions, screams and laughter.

What a whiff!

The next evening, Mum was wiping the tears from her eyes.

"I think we'd best leave you to it," she said.

Dad was bound in a red-and-white cloth and was dripping with a pale green juice! Bits of leaves clung to his forehead and water sprang from his eyes! An old, hunched woman in a brightly patterned shawl picked up her potions and put them in her carpet bag.

"Thank you, Chelti Gamra," said Nanna. "*Insha'Allah*, your potion will help."

The old lady smiled. "*Insha'Allah*. And may your futures all be blessed," she said. The heels of her shoes clattered down the stone staircase as Nanna showed her to the door.

Mum swirled a sparkling yellow hijab round her hair and tied it under her chin. "Right," she said, holding her nose. "Is dere anydig you want before we go out for sub fresh air?"

Dad sneezed and wiped the tears from his eyes. "I'll be fine," he sighed.

Ramzi went over to kiss Dad goodbye, but quickly changed his mind. "Dad! You stink!" he cried.

"Just you wait!" shouted Dad.

But Mum and Ramzi didn't. They just ran out of the door!

***

Nanna and Uncle Kader were sitting outside. There was an old tin bucket on the doorstep. Ramzi peered inside. Then he jumped back.

"Do you want to set fire to it?" asked Uncle Kader.

"OK," said Ramzi.. "But is it already totally dead?"

"It's only the skin," smiled Uncle Kader. He handed Ramzi a box of matches. Ramzi felt excited. He wasn't allowed even to touch matches at home.

As he dropped the burning flame into the bucket, a strange green smoke swirled into the air. The snake skin fizzled like a firework.

"Wow!" exclaimed Ramzi.

the snake skin is inside

"That should scare away any evil spirits," said Uncle Kader.

Nanna nodded her head. She looked serious.

"But will it work?" asked Ramzi.

"If God wills it," replied Nanna. "My brother used to burn a snake skin in the middle of our flock of sheep at sunset. It always kept the wolves away."

"Wow!" said Ramzi again.

"Let's hope it scares away Mohamed's bad dreams," laughed Mum. "Snake skins – who'd have thought. . ."

"He doesn't have bad dreams when he's here with

me," snapped Nanna. She sounded cross. Picking up her cushion, she went back upstairs.

"Oh dear," sighed Mum. "I hope I haven't upset … it's just… well, you see, I've never burnt snake skins before and…"

"Take no notice," said Uncle Kader. "*Yemma* just misses Mohamed. He was *always* her favourite."

"But she's right," said Mum sadly. "He doesn't have bad dreams when he's here."

They all looked at the bucket in silence and listened to the snake skin crackle.

***

When Ramzi went back upstairs, the sharp smell of herbs and onions made his eyes sting.

"Has Uncle Kader burnt the snake skin yet?" asked Dad. His sweating head was resting against Nanna's knee.

"Yeh, Dad. It was completely brilliant! I set it on fire and the smoke was bright green!"

Dad smiled. His cheeks were flushed and his eyes were watering.

Nanna took off her white shawl and arranged

it carefully on Dad's pillow. Then she stroked his forehead with her star-tattooed hand and began to tell Dad a story.

"It is called *The Keys of Destiny*," she began, "It is written, Oh Auspicious King...."

Ramzi listened, spellbound, for what seemed like forever. He didn't want the story to stop.

But then Nanna said, "At that moment, Scheherazade saw the approach of the morning and discreetly fell silent."

"That was brilliant, Nanna," sighed Ramzi. But something Nanna had said had made him feel uneasy

. . . Scheherazade . . . Scheherazade . . . Suddenly, he remembered that night in the woods! The fire. The tisane. The prophecy. What if Boulelli was right? What if only *Ramzi* could help Dad? What if the wise-man's remedies failed?

"Dad," Ramzi blurted out. "What if the wise-man's cure doesn't work?"

"It will!" said Dad.

"But…" began Ramzi.

"But nothing!" snapped Dad. He wiped the sweat off his forehead. "God save us from the fire," he muttered to himself.

Suddenly, there were noises outside.

BOOM, BOOM, BOOM, went the gunshots in the streets!

"*Ulo, ulo, ulo, ulo!*" cried the women.

BANG, BANG, BANG, went the drums.

"It's another wedding," smiled Nanna.

As Ramzi looked at Dad resting on the pillow next to Nanna, an idea slowly formed in his mind.

Sighs and Sadness

During the last few days in the town that never slept, something strange happened to time. It began to speed up. At first, no one noticed. Nanna burnt her biscuits, Uncle Kader overslept and Mum missed some of her prayers. They couldn't understand why.

But Dad knew. "It's the time!" he said. "It's going too fast." He tried standing still and staring at the clock. But that didn't slow it down. Nothing could.

On the last night, Ramzi was outside with Meccy and Amel. "I wish I'd had time to say goodbye to the Spider."

"Can you stay for another week?" asked Amel.

Ramzi shrugged his shoulders.

"I don't want you to go," cried Meccy. "I hate Cinnamon Grove. Stay here."

Amel put her arm around Meccy's shoulders and wiped his eyes with her sleeve.

"I'll email. Dad's got skype. It'll be cool," said Ramzi. His words sounded hollow. "You could visit? Maybe next year?"

They nodded and smiled. But they weren't real smiles. And Ramzi knew why. He'd heard Uncle Kader and Dad shouting downstairs.

"*England?* It's easier to get into Paradise!"

But perhaps they'd get a visa, one day? The air was heavy with sighs and sadness and everyone looked glum.

As night fell, a rickety truck turned into the street. Its juddering headlights flashed in the darkness and made Ramzi close his eyes and turn away. In the shadows, some figures bustled into Nanna Ramadan's house.

"Come on," called Amel excitedly. "It's the Zidanes. They're hardly ever in town. They must have come to say goodbye."

"*More* cousins?" asked Ramzi. "Are you sure?"

"Yeh," grinned Meccy, skipping up the echoing staircase.

Amel was right. The Zidanes had come to wish the Ramadans farewell. But Dad wasn't ready to say goodbye and Mum hadn't even packed. So whilst

Mum gathered up crunchy socks from the moonlit
sun terrace and faded towels from the balcony,
everyone squeezed into the lounge to hear stories
about Dad when he was a boy.

***

Just after sunrise, Uncle Kader's yellow car was
waiting outside in the street – its little engine
throbbing in the crisp morning air. Aunts and
uncles, neighbours and cousins, shopkeepers and
teachers, even the local policeman, had all come to
say goodbye.

"Come on, Ramzi," called Mum. "If we don't go now, we'll miss the plane!"

"Thanks, Nanna," said Ramzi. He kissed Nanna on both cheeks and stuffed something into his rucksack.

Nanna hugged him until he could hardly breathe. Then she took off one of her gold bracelets and squeezed it on to Mum's wrist. "Come back soon, my English bride," she said.

Mum hugged Nanna.

"May you live for ever, *Yemma*," said Dad, blinking back tears.

Nanna picked up her long, flowery dress and hurried back inside.

They left the little town on the orange rock and travelled back through the salt marshes and purple mountains. Mum, Ramzi and Uncle Kader chatted away but Dad remained strangely silent.

When they arrived at the airport, they said their goodbyes and dragged their heavy cases towards the terminal.

"Ramzi – I nearly forgot," shouted Uncle Kader. "You asked for this." He leant over the barrier and gave a small parcel to Ramzi.

"Thanks, Uncle Kader," said Ramzi, putting it into his bag. Then he ran to catch up with Mum and Dad and disappeared into the bustling crowds. Only the straight-backed soldiers watched as the little yellow car drove away.

the parcel

Snakes in the Jungle

Back at Cinnamon Grove, nothing had changed. The air was fresh, the sun was gentle and Ramzi could breathe again. He delivered bright packets of Turkish Delight to all of his friends and played football on the wet, green grass. Mum took boxes of glistening dates round to all the neighbours and gave the Stalks their brightly coloured scarves. Meanwhile, Dad played Berber music and steamed couscous in the kitchen.

On Monday morning, Mum and Dad went back to work and Ramzi returned to school. And so the weeks passed. Peacefully quiet and still.

But then, one night, something happened ...

***

"ARGHHHHHH!!!!" came a high-pitched scream from the bedroom. It was Mum. "Mohamed, what in Heaven's name?" she shrieked.

"What is it?" cried Dad, as he leapt out of bed.

Ramzi ran across the landing. "Oh no, Dad!" he gasped.

"What's the problem? I was sleeping... *I'm cured,*" shouted Dad.

Mum said nothing. But then a tiny noise came out of her mouth. "Ah," she squeaked.

"What is it?" asked Dad.

"Dad," said Ramzi gently. "Just look at your feet."

Dad looked down and jumped back in horror. He was wearing a pair of muddy green wellington boots! He shook them off as if they were snakes in the jungle.

Mum stared at the sticky brown trail that led across the carpet and on to the bed sheets. Dad looked at it too. Then he sank down on the edge of the bed and buried his face his hands.

"It hasn't worked," he groaned. "We've only been back a few weeks and my sleepwalking has returned!"

Mum sat down next to him. Ramzi sat on the

other side. They put their arms round Dad but he couldn't be consoled.

"Whilst I am a foreigner in this cold, wet country," he said, "my dreams will always torment me."

"Don't be silly," said Mum. "You're *not* a foreigner. You're my wonderful, clever, brilliant Mohamed Ramadan, computer wizard and father extraordinaire!" Mum's bottom lip quivered as she spoke.

Dad stared blankly at the footprints on the carpet and listened to the alarm clock tick.

But Ramzi looked thoughtful. The wise-man *had* failed. Boulelli's prophecy must be right: *only the boy can save his father from his nightmares.*

It was time to put the plan into action.

Ramzi's Midnight Plan

After school the next day, Ramzi asked if he could go and see Shaima. Dad was in the kitchen, his head slumped on the kitchen table.

"Ask your mother," he grunted.

Mum said Ramzi could go, so he ran up the street and knocked on Shaima's door.

Mr Stalk answered. He was wearing a beige *salwar kameez* and had wonky front teeth and a friendly smile.

"You must be the famous Ramzi Ramadan! *Assalemu aleikum*, come in!" he said. The house smelt warm and cosy – all lemony soap and spice.

Ramzi said "*Salem*", took off his shoes and followed Mr Stalk into the lounge. The Stalk family were sitting cross-legged on the floor.

"I win!" shouted Nanna Stalk gleefully. She slung the end of her sequin-speckled sari over her shoulder and waved a hand at Ramzi. Ramzi waved shyly back. Shaima's little brother, Iqbal, didn't turn round. He was too busy balancing the egg-timer on his head.

"Hi, Ramzi," said Shaima, "We're playing Boggle. Do you want to join in?"

"Ermm…" began Ramzi.

"Another time," said Shaima, standing up. "Nanna always wins anyway!"

"Why don't you two come with me and I'll make you some fresh mango juice," said Mrs Stalk, getting to her feet. "Ramzi looks all worn out!"

So Shaima and Ramzi followed her into the kitchen and sat at the table and waited. The room smelt different to the hall – sort of coconut milk and cardamom. Ramzi sniffed deeply and sighed.

"You look terrible, Ramzi! What's up?" whispered Shaima.

"It's Dad," replied Ramzi. "He's sleepwalking again."

"I thought you said the wise-man had cured him?"

Ramzi shrugged his shoulders.

"So the Spider was right!" whispered Shaima. "I knew it! And you've got a plan?"

Ramzi's eyes glistened. "Yes, actually, I have," he said. "I just need to borrow something. Have you got an MP3 player?"

But Shaima was already running upstairs to fetch it.

"Stop running about like an elephant!" shouted Mrs Stalk.

"Sorry, Mum," yelled Shaima. She clattered down the stairs and handed it to Ramzi. "Good luck," she said, and she winked.

"Thanks." Ramzi wiped the juice from around his mouth and said goodbye to the Stalk family.

"Why didn't you ask him what he needed it for?" asked Mrs Stalk.

But Shaima just smiled. She already knew.

***

That night, for the first time ever, Dad *didn't* come to say good night. So Ramzi curled up in bed, stared into the darkness and waited. He thought about the parcel from Uncle Kader. He thought about Scheherazade, Meccy and Amel. And he thought about Nanna Ramadan . . .

At last, there was a *click* as Dad opened the front door. Mum was already asleep. Ramzi listened as Dad moved about downstairs. Eventually, Dad turned off the lights and went to bed. Ramzi waited. And waited.

When he was sure that Dad was asleep, Ramzi crept across the landing. He was carrying Nanna's white shawl and Shaima's MP3 player. Doubt flooded his mind. Would the files that he'd copied from Uncle Kader's flash disc work? He pushed open the door and stopped. Dad mumbled something. Ramzi held his breath.

"I'm falling, I'm falling," muttered Dad. His head lurched sideways.

With trembling hands, Ramzi spread Nanna's white shawl across Dad's pillow. A strange smell of onions and herbs filled the air. Dad flung his arm across the bed and moved his head back to where it had been.

Very carefully, Ramzi placed the headphones on Dad's ears. Then he touched 'PLAY' and selected 'CONTINUOUS'. Dad grunted quietly. Ramzi stepped away from the bed and out of the room.

In the light cast from the landing, Ramzi watched as a curious smile spread across Dad's face.

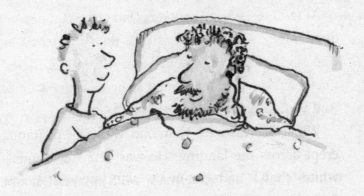

"Allah – Please make Dad better," whispered Ramzi. Then he crept back to his own bed and turned out the light.

Sweet Dreams?

Ever since Ramzi had put his plan into action, the Spider's prophecy had come true. A year had passed and there had been *no* frogs in the pantry, boat trips to the moon or hens in the wardrobe. There had been *no* snow-leopards in the treetops, wellies in the bed sheets or fire engines in the night! In fact, all was quiet in Cinnamon Grove....

The little cluster of grey terraced houses huddled together beneath the moonlight. Birds tucked their heads under their wings, flowers closed their petals, and children snuggled into their duvets like caterpillars in cocoons. Only the brook that gurgled along the bottom of the gardens interrupted the sleepy silence. Everything was drifting into the deep hush of night.

Suddenly, there was a noise at Number Thirty-two!

Waaaaaaaa, Waaaaaaaa, Waaaaaaaaa.

An upstairs light came on, a door swung open and Mum hurtled across the landing. She burst into a tiny bedroom and stopped.

Ramzi was standing by a wooden cot, a bundle of blankets in his arms. "It's OK, Mum," he beamed.

"You go back to bed. I'll rock Scheherazade to sleep."

A tiny face looked up at Ramzi and blew bubbles out of her cherry-pink lips. Ramzi kissed her on the forehead. "Sweet dreams, Baby Zed." She gurgled and said "coooo". Ramzi laughed.

Mum tiptoed dreamily back to her bedroom. As she walked past Dad, she paused. Dad's head rested on Nanna's white shawl as it spread across his pillow. A pair of black headphones sat snugly on his head. Mum lent over and listened.

"BOOM, BOOM, BOOM," went the gunshots in the streets!

"ULO, ULO, ULO, ULO, ULO, ULO," cried the women.

"BANG, BANG, BANG!" went the drums.

In the air, there was a faint smell of onions. Mum looked back at Ramzi and smiled.

This *was* the best of all possible worlds.

At last Dad felt at home and he was sleeping like a baby.

the
best
of
all
possible
worlds

the end

What things Mean
by Ramzi Ramadan

Ablutions

This is a special wash we do before prayer – it's really tricky to learn as you have to wash your hands, mouth, nose, face, arms, hair, ears and feet: three times each and in the right order.

Alhamdulillah

I always say this when I score a penalty or get an extra slice of chocolate cake. It means *Thanks be to God.*

Allahu akbar

This is the Arabic way of saying *God is greater (than everything)* and it is how the call to prayer always starts.

Assalemu aleikum

This means *Peace be upon you.* It sounds a bit funny in English but it's really cool in Arabic. It's a bit like saying, "Hi, I'm a friend and it's great to see you," all at once.

Astaghfirullah

This is something you say when you've done something silly or wrong. It means *God forgive me* and grown-ups mumble it under their breath quite a lot.

Bismillah

I always say this before I eat. You can say it before you do anything though, because it makes you feel stronger inside. It means *In the Name of God*.

Fajr prayer

This is the really early prayer – the one *before* the sun comes up. Muslims do five prayers a day and they all have different names. I don't do all five yet but Shaima does.

Hijab

In Arabic, *hijab* means *cover* but people here use it to mean a Muslim headscarf. My mum wears one some of the time but Mrs Stalk wears one all of the time. Mrs Stalk's headscarves have glittery tassels and look really cool. Mum's keep slipping off.

Insha'Allah

This means *God willing*. So, if Dad says "I'm not getting stuck up a tree again", I say "Insha'Allah".

Jilbab

A kind of long gown-type thing that lots of Muslim women wear over their real clothes. Mum has a stripy green-and-silver one that she wears for parties. Mrs Stalk wears hers every day but only when she goes outside. (Inside, she dresses really fancy: all gold bracelets and sparkly stuff. Mum doesn't. She just wears jeans.)

Masha'Allah

When old ladies think my curls are cute (yuck), they say "Hasn't he got beautiful hair, Masha'Allah?" It means *As God willed*.

Minaret

This is the tall bit of the mosque, and loads of storks make their nests in them.

Salem

This means *Peace*. It's like saying "Hi". Sort of.

Scheherazade
This looks hard to say but it isn't. *Shuh-hair-a-zed*. See?
Easy.

Subhan'Allah
If Nanna Ramadan spoke English, she'd say something
like *"God is glorious"*. But she doesn't. She only speaks
Berber and Arabic. So she says *"Subhan'Allah"*.

Ululating
This is a funny warbling noise that lots of women in
the world do when they're excited - mostly at weddings
and parties. My nanna is brilliant at it. She rolls her
tongue in the back of her throat and sings a really
high-pitched note. "Ulalalalalalalalala . . ." When I try
and do it, Shaima just laughs.

Yemma
This is what Dad calls Nanna Ramadan – but he always
says it softly and holds her hand at the same time.
I think it means 'Mum' and some more special things
all rolled up in one word.

Nana Ramadan's Special Crunchy biscuits!

crumbs

You will need:

4 eggs

350g (1.5 cups) sugar

1 cup of vegetable oil

1 tsp vanilla essence

500g (2 cups) self-raising flour

Some sesame seeds

A large baking tray, a bowl, a wooden spoon

- Mix the eggs, sugar, vegetable oil and vanilla essence together in a big bowl.

- Add the flour and mix together with a big wooden spoon.

- Lightly grease a large baking tray.

- Pour the mixture in. Pat down with oily hands until flat.

- Sprinkle some sesame seeds on the top.

- Cook in the oven at 180c, Gas mark 4.

- When the mixture becomes a bit firm, slice into rectangular biscuit shapes. Cook until crunchy.

Nanna Ramadan's top tip: if you want your biscuits to look shiny, brush over the top with beaten egg midway through cooking.

THE BEST BIT!
Eat with warm milk or freshly picked peppermint tea!

* eat quickly before some one else does!
(and don't forget to say 'Bismillah')

ACKNOWLEDGEMENTS

Lots of wonderful people helped me to write this book – even if they didn't know it!

My parents – who read to me as a child and inspired my love of stories
My children – who made me laugh and shared me with my lap-top
My Berber family-in-law – who took me into their hearts
My friends – who made me coffee and helped me meet my deadlines
My designer – who brought out the best in my illustrations

And finally, special thanks go to my patient and generous editor – Janetta Otter-Barry – who let me tell my story but made sure that I did it well.

WENDY MEDDOUR

As a child, Wendy spent most of her time
in the airing cupboard reading books. Huddled up
behind the boiler, she dreamt of being a cartoonist,
a comedienne and a football player. Unsure
how to go about it, she became an English lecturer
instead—one that gave funny lectures, doodled
in the margins and knew the off-side rule.
Since leaving the safety of the airing cupboard,
she has acquired a doctorate, an Algerian husband,
four children, a wobbly old house in Wiltshire,
a farm in the Berber mountains and a huge cat
called Socrates (that many suspect is actually a goat).
Wendy's début novel, *A Hen in the Wardrobe,*
has already garnered critical success – winning
the John C. Laurence Award for writing that
improves relations between races, taking first place
in the Islamic Foundation's International Writing
Competition, and being shortlisted for
the Muslim Writer's Award 2011.

**Look out for the next funny adventure
in the CINNAMON GROVE series
coming soon…**

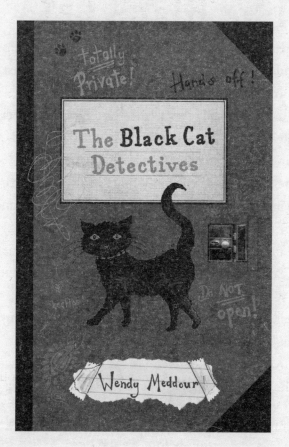

The Black Cat Detectives

**Something suspicious is going on
in Cinnamon Grove...**

Auntie Urooj, world-famous beetle expert, is lonely
and Ramzi and his friend Shaima Stalk think
they have the perfect solution – a suitor from
Truly Deeply Muslims online marriage agency!
But smooth-talking Rasheed is not what he seems.
He cheats at Monopoly for a start, and pretends
to be an orphan...
It's time for action. Ramzi and Shaima set up
the Black Cat Detective Agency to find out all about
Rasheed and his dastardly plot. Can they rescue
Auntie Urooj and her deeply endangered beetle
collection before it's too late?
A funny and exciting mystery story from
the author of *A Hen in the Wardrobe*

Winner of the 2009 inaugural FRANCES LINCOLN
DIVERSE VOICES CHILDREN'S BOOK AWARD for an
outstanding debut novel celebrating cultural diversity.

TAKESHITA DEMONS

Cristy Burne

Illustrated by Siku

Miku knows she's in trouble when her substitute
teacher turns out to be a Nukekubi – a bloodthirsty
demon who can turn into a flying head and whose
favourite snack is children. That night, in a raging
snowstorm, Miku's baby brother Kazu is kidnapped by
the demons, and then it's up to Miku and
her friend Cait to get him back. Can they outwit the
faceless Nopera-bo? Is the dragon-like Woman of the
Wet a force for good or evil? And then there's the
Nukekubi herself, on the rampage
and ready to attack. . .

Praise for Takeshita Demons:
"A gripping, superbly written debut novel" *Writeaway*

Takeshita Demons:
THE FILTH LICKER
Cristy Burne
Illustrated by Siku

School Camp should have been a fun week. But Miku feels something is terribly wrong. And that's before Oscar gets a festering rash on the bus, before an eerie wind blows out the camp bonfire and before Alex finds the frog-like, red-clawed Filth Licker in the boys' toilets...

In the forest, where nothing and no one are what they seem, Cait, Alex and Miku meet the Shape-Shifters – a mind-reading, stinking giant monkey, a pyromaniac fox with three tails and, most horrifying, the blood-eating Sickle Weasels, the kama itachi, with their lethal sickle blades.

Can Miku save herself and her friends? And what about the Filth Licker? Whose side is he really on?

Winner of the FRANCES LINCOLN
DIVERSE VOICES CHILDREN'S BOOK AWARD 2011

TOO MUCH TROUBLE

Tom Avery

"Get out, Emmanuel!" growled my uncle.
"Take your brother and go."

But where can two boys go when they're on their own,
on the run, with little money or food? All 12-year-old
Emmanuel knows is that he has to look after Prince.
Those were his father's last words to him.

On the train to London, Em and Prince have no idea
where they will end up but then they meet
the mysterious Mr Green and his 'friends'. And that's
when things start to spin out of control.

"This action-packed, contemporary Oliver Twist story
is a real page-turner." Trevor Phillips, Diverse Voices
Award judge and Chair, Equality and
Human Rights Commission